SCAVENGERS

Blade swung into action the moment he saw Jared's hand sweep toward the holster. He lunged to his left, his huge arm encircling Jenny and Gabe, bearing them to the ground, shielding them from the anticipated shot. Expecting to feel a searing pain as the slug tore through him, he twisted as he went down, training the Commando on the scavengers. He could see Jared sighting the Smith and Wesson, apparently intent on making an accurate shot, but the revolver wasn't aiming at Blade, Jenny or Gabe.

The scavenger was pointing the gun at something behind them.

A snarling form hurdled over the Warrior and his family, springing at the scavengers. The Smith and Wesson boomed, but the shot missed. Before Jared could fire again, a feral feline landed on all fours, uttered a piercing, raspy scream of rage, and launched itself at one of the scavengers. . . .

ALSO IN THE *BLADE* SERIES:

- #1: FIRST STRIKE
- #2: OUTLANDS STRIKE
- #3: VAMPIRE STRIKE
- #4: PIPELINE STRIKE
- #5: PIRATE STRIKE
- #6: CRUSHER STRIKE

BLADE
#7: TERROR STRIKE
DAVID ROBBINS

LEISURE BOOKS   NEW YORK CITY

Dedicated to
Judy, Joshua and Shane.
To Sylvester Stallone, who demonstrated the
value of persistence.
To Scott and Fran Charles, for dedication above
and beyond the call of duty.
And to Jerry and Linda Jeffries, who give the word
friendship its true meaning.

A LEISURE BOOK®

April 1990

Dorchester Publishing Co., Inc.
276 Fifth Avenue
New York, NY 10001

Copyright ©1990 by David L. Robbins

All rights reserved. No part of this book may be reproduced or transmitted in any form or by any electronic or mechanical means, including photocopying, recording, or by any information storage and retrieval system, without the written permission of the Publisher, except where permitted by law.

The name "Leisure Books" and the stylized "L" with design are trademarks of Dorchester Publishing Co., Inc.

Printed in the United States of America.

PROLOGUE

"Where the hell are we?"

"Beats me."

"You're a lot of help."

"Hey, you're the jerk who lost the map."

The two grungy men halted and glared at each other. Both stood about six feet in height, and both were lean and sinewy. One had blond hair, the other black, and both had brown eyes. The blond wore a ragged green shirt and faded, torn jeans, while his companion was attired in a dirty brown short-sleeved shirt and patched blue corduroy pants that had seen their prime a century earlier. The men's footware consisted of crudely made deerskin shoes.

"Who are you calling a jerk?" the blond demanded angrily, his hands tightening on the Remington Model Seven rifle he held.

"There's no one else within miles of here, Merrill," the man in the corduroy pants said. Cradled in his arms was a Beeman/Krico Model Six Hundred, and strapped to his left hip a Caspian Arms .45-caliber pistol.

"It wasn't my fault the damn map slipped out of my back pocket," Merrill said, and frowned.

"You were carrying it."

"Get off my case, Emerson," Merill snapped. He turned and headed due south, moving down the slope of the low hill they were on.

"Boy, are you in a lousy mood," Emerson said, following.

"No thanks to you, turkey," Merrill shot back over his left shoulder.

"I didn't lose the map," Emerson said.

"No, but this stupid plan was your idea, not mine."

"My plan was sound."

Merrill snorted derisively, his eyes scanning the waist-high vegetation in front of him and the forest less than 50 yards distant. "Sure it was."

"So my information was unreliable," Emerson said. "Shoot me."

"Don't tempt me," Merrill replied.

"I believed the gambler in Shantytown when he told us about Canada," Emerson said wistfully.

"You believed his story about Canada being unaffected by World War Three? About Canada hardly being touched by the radiation, the chemicals, and all that other crap?"

"Well, I—" Emerson began.

"You actually believed his tale about cities teeming with people, about cities where they still have cars that run, and food can be bought at stores, and there's electricity and running water and everyone has a roof over their heads?" Merrill asked resentfully.

Emerson sighed. "It could've been true."

"Yeah. Right. Just like the stories we've heard about California, the Civilized Zone, and Miami could also be true," Merrill said sarcastically, and stopped. He faced Emerson. "When will you learn? You know as well as I do that those stories are all a load of bull. There's no truth to any of them. People wish it was true, because everyone yearns for the good old days when living was easy, when all a person had to do to get light was flick a switch, or if they were hungry they went to a store and bought all the food they needed." He paused. "But things aren't that way any more. The war threw everything out of whack. If we want to eat, we have to kill game or trade for provisions at Shantytown or one of the other rat-infested towns. If we want light, we have to build a fire or use a lantern."

"There are generators in use," Emerson said lamely.

"Yeah. A few here and there. So what? A few generators don't change the fact that you're always chasing pipe dreams. You think we're going to find paradise, a city exactly like those in existence before the war. It won't happen."

"You never know."

"I know you're crazy, and I know I'm tired of going with you on these wild-goose chases."

"Answer me this, then, Mister-Know-It-All. If you're so smart, if you're positive that cities like those before the war don't exist, then how come you go with me all the time? How come you offered to go with me to Miami, even though we changed our minds when we found out we'd have to go through the Russian sector? And how come you came with me on this trip to Canada?"

Merrill shook his head and resumed his trek. "Because I'm your friend, your dipstick."

They hiked in silence for several minutes.

"I'm sorry I got on you about the map," Emerson said.

"You should be."

"Look, I'm trying to apologize and you're treating me like dirt."

"No, I'm treating you like a chump. There's a difference."

"I'm a chump?"

"We both are," Merrill stated bitterly. "We've always been chumps. From the day we were born in run-down shacks near what's left of Duluth, we've been busting our butts to get ahead. And what has all our effort got us? Nothing. Zip. The clothes on our backs and our guns. That's it."

"We're still friends after all these years."

"Yeah. When we were kids, living within a half mile of one another, I never figured I'd be seeing your ugly mug every day twenty years later."

"Don't you want to be friends any longer?"

Merrill gazed at the western horizon. "What I want is to find us a place to bed down for the night. We have about two hours of daylight left."

"There's plenty of time," Emerson said.

"There you go again."

"What am I doing?"

"Being your usual, disgusting, optimistic self."

In short order they came to the forest and discovered a game trail winding in the direction they were heading.

"Let's take it," Emerson proposed.

An eerie hush enveloped the pair as they wound among the trees. No insects sounds could be heard, and the birds, if there were any, were strangely silent. Even the breeze was silent.

"This is spooky," Emerson said softly.

"Maybe there's a bear or a bobcat in the vicinity," Merrill suggested.

"Maybe there's a mutation."

The dreaded word made Merrill stroke the trigger on his rifle nervously. He despised the vile genetic abominations so prevalent since the nuclear holocaust, and the mere thought of a two-headed wolf or an enormous snake lurking in the undergrowth gave him goose bumps. He couldn't begin to imagine what life had been like prior to the war, before the radiation and the chemicals had polluted the environment and deranged the wildlife. Once, in International Falls, he'd spoken to a man who claimed the "warping of the ecological chain" meant all future generations would have to contend with a world overrun by mutants, which was a disheartening scenario if ever there was one.

"This game trail might lead us to water," Emerson commented.

Merrill nodded. Game trails usually did, sooner or later, lead to water. The animals used the trails like ancient men

TERROR STRIKE

and women had once used their roads and highways.

"We must be in northern Minnesota," Emerson mentioned.

"That'd be my guess," Merrill concurred. Their swing into Canadian territory, which they had entered near Fort Frances, had taken them northward, around the Lake of the Woods, then to the west, encompassing hundreds of miles and three months. And all for nothing. Their search for an inhabited Canadian metropolis had been fruitless. Oh, they'd found a few towns inhabited by trappers and hunters, but not the utopian city they were seeking. If Emerson had had his way, they would still be looking. The dummy had wanted them to try and push on to Winnipeg, but Merrill had put his foot down and refused to continue.

"I don't want to sleep in these woods," Emerson stated nervously.

"Then you'd better hope we get out of these trees before nightfall," Merrill said.

In a quarter of a mile they did. The forest abruptly ended at the edge of a field. Beyond the field, in an oval configuration aligned from north to south, was a small lake, its deep blue surface tranquil, the sunlight shimmering on the water.

"Fish for supper!" Emerson declared.

"We'll camp right next to the lake," Merrill said, then glanced to the right. "What the hell!"

"What?" Emerson responded, looking around.

Not thirty feet away, situated close to the trees, was an old log cabin, its roof and glass windows still intact.

"Will you look at that!" Merrill exclaimed happily.

"Do you suppose someone lives there?"

"There's only one way to find out."

They approached the structure warily, circling to the front on the south side, their rifles trained on the closed door.

"I doubt anyone has lived there in years, maybe since the war," Merrill speculated.

"If it's empty we can spend the night inside," Emerson said.

"Open the door," Merrill directed.

"You open it."

"What's the matter? Chicken?"

"No."

"We're not in the woods any more," Merrill stated.

"Meaning what?" Emerson asked.

"Meaning you're having a bad attack of nerves, and the best way for you to get over the willies is to go open the damn door," Merrill said. "I'll cover you."

"Okay. Okay. Don't rush me." Emerson edged closer and closer to the cabin, his eyes flicking over the two windows, one to the right and the other to the left of the door. He held the Beeman at waist level.

"Hurry it up. We don't have all day," Merrill snapped.

Emerson ignored him and moved to the door. He grasped the knob with his right hand, twisted, and shoved, then crouched, braced for the worst. The door swung inward to reveal a room that hadn't been occupied in decades. Dust covered everything. A sofa was positioned along the west wall. Shelves crammed with books lined the east wall. A blue shag rug covered the floor. In the center of the room stood a rocking chair, a straight chair, and a coffee table between the two.

"Anything?" Merrill inquired.

Emerson stepped inside. In the northwest corner was a kitchenette complete with a wood-burning stove and a rack containing an assortment of dishes. Across from the kitchen area was an open door.

"Anything?" Merrill repeated.

Without answering, Emerson walked to the open door and peered into a narrow bedroom in which there were three items of furniture: a bed, a dresser, and a nightstand.

Merrill came into the front room. "I asked you a question."

"I heard you."

"Then why didn't you respond?"

"Because I'm tired of you riding herd over me today," Emerson said, stepping to the sofa and sitting down. "No one died and made you boss. We're partners, remember?"

"Hey, I wasn't trying to upset you," Merrill said.

"Too bad. You did a good job."

Merrill glanced down at their footprints on the dusty carpet. "What did I tell you? Nobody has been here in ages."

"It's been one hundred and six years since the war. Do you think this cabin has been abandoned that long?"

"Who can say?" Merrill replied, and moved to the kitchenette. "Do you still want to spend the night?"

"The night, hell. Let's take a week off and relax."

"Fine by me. But if we're going to have fish for supper, one of us had better get to fishing while the other does the cleaning. I don't intend to breathe dust the whole week."

Emerson rose. "Okay. I'll do the fishing."

"Let's pick for it."

"All right," Emerson said. He reached into his right front pocket and extracted a bullet, then placed the Beeman on the sofa. Hiding his hands behind his back, he palmed the cartridge in his left hand. "Ready?"

"I was born ready."

Emerson extended his arms, fists clenched. "Pick the one."

"Now which hand has it?" Merrill asked rhetorically, and scratched the stubble on his chin.

"You'll never guess."

"The left one."

Dejected, Emerson opened his left hand, disclosing the bullet. "Damn. How'd you know?"

"Simple. You took it out of your pocket with your right hand, and I just figured you'd naturally transfer it to your left," Merrill said, and smirked triumphantly. He strolled to the front door. "I'll be back in an hour with more fish than we'll need. Try to have the place dusted out by then."

"Don't rub it in."

Merrill snickered.

"Hey, wait," Emerson declared.

"We're not going to pick two out of three," Merrill stated.

"Not that. Look," Emerson said, and pointed at the southwest corner.

Merrill pivoted and spied the closet. "Now what do you suppose is in there?"

"Let's see."

They converged on the closet and Merrill opened the door.

"Wow! Will you look at that!" Emerson exclaimed.

The previous owner had filled the closet with camping, hunting, and fishing gear, including two fishing poles leaning against the left wall.

"There aren't any guns, but these will do nicely," Merrill said, and withdrew the poles. He propped the shorter of the pair against the door and hefted a black and white model fitted with a black reel. "Now I won't have to use the roll of wire in my pocket."

"I get the other pole."

"It's yours. But you don't get to use it until the cabin is cleaned. A deal is a deal."

"Crap," Emerson said.

Merrill smiled and exited. He slung the Remington over his right shoulder and made for the lake, experimenting with the rod and reel as he went. He'd never seen a fishing pole in such superb condition! And now it was his! He toyed with the idea of taking the pole to Shantytown and trading the rod for a week of women and wine, but he discarded the brainstorm after concluding there were more important things in life than a week in the sack with a wench. Like fishing.

Once again he noticed the quiet in the air, and he paused to gaze at the forest to his rear. Nothing moved. Not even a leaf or a pine needle.

Damn! He was getting as bad as Emerson!

Eager to try out the new rod, Merrill hastened to the lake shore, a narrow strip of dirt ringing the water. He wondered if the line would hold up as he unfastened the hook from the top. His first step was to dig some worms. He looked at the cabin, approximately 20 yards from the water, and saw Emerson moving about inside.

Something splashed in the lake.

Merrill turned and saw the ripples where something had broken the surface and then submerged, and prompted by his hunger he walked along the shore, seeking a suitable spot to dig. In 15 yards he found a moist, soft track of soil and began scooping out the dirt with his hands. At a depth of two inches the familiar form of a nice, juicy worm squiggled into view. He plucked the bait from the soil and proceeded to slowly insert the hook.

Another splash left concentric wavelets on the lake.

The worm wriggled violently, resisting the impaling.

Merrill applied more pressure with his right thumb and forefinger and finished preparing the bait. He hefted the pole, admiring its balance, and inspected the reel. In comparison to the wire and any thin tree limb he ordinarily employed, the fishing pole was exotic and alien. He knew nothing about operating the reel. There must be, he reasoned, a method of unwinding the line smoothly. He saw a red button with three distinct settings, and he switched from one setting to another, testing the rod.

Yet another splash sounded, this time much nearer.

The prospect of hauling in a tasty bass or trout caused Merrill's stomach to growl. Unsure of how to cast the pole and afraid of tangling the line, he unwound 20 feet, backing away from the sinker as he did. Then he swung the pole in an arc overhead, the line whipping through the air, and brought his arm down when the pole pointed directly over the lake. To his amazement, the line not only sailed out over the water, it kept going, the reel spinning and buzzing like an angry bee, until the sinker plopped into the lake almost 40 feet from where he stood.

Terrific!

Merrill chuckled and settled down to await the first nibble. Within minutes a fish took the bait, and after a brief, exciting contest, Merrill reeled in a feisty lake trout 18 inches in length. Encouraged by his success, he spent the next 40 minutes fishing, hauling in seven healthy specimens for the supper table. He used a short piece of wire, tied to a stout section of tree branch he found next to the lake, to rig a string for his catch. The sun was sinking below the western horizon when he ambled to the cabin, holding the fish in his left hand.

The cabin door was open.

"Emerson! I hope you're hungry," Merrill declared as he entered the cabin. "Look at what we have."

Engaged in checking the fire he'd kindled in the wood-burning stove, Emerson looked up and beamed. "Wow! Did they jump into your arms?"

"No. My superior fishing skill caught them."

"I don't suppose the new rod helped?" Emerson asked, rising.

"It's incredible," Merrill admitted, surveying the furniture and the floor. "Hey, you got rid of all the dust."

"I found a broom in a closet in the bedroom."

"Then let's get to feeding our faces," Merrill proposed.

They set about preparing the fish. The delicious aroma of their simmering supper filled the cabin. Merrill closed the cabin door.

Emerson arranged plates and glasses on the kitchen counter. "Look at what else I found," he mentioned, and reached into a cabinet on the north wall to produce salt and pepper shakers.

"Is that real salt?" Merrill queried.

"You bet."

Merrill could hardly wait to tear into their meal. Salt was a luxury in postwar America, and a bag or bottle of the condiment could be worth its weight in gold to an astute trader. His mouth salivated in anticipation.

"Did I show you this?" Emerson mentioned, and leaned down to tug on the knob on a cupboard located to the left of the sink. The three shelves inside the cupboard were stacked high with canned goods.

"We must've died and gone to heaven," Merrill said.

"I say we stay here for a month, at least."

"It's only the end of May. Why don't we stay until the end of summer? We don't have anything else to do."

Emerson nodded and closed the cupboard. "Why not? We have all the comforts. I found lanterns, kerosene, matches, all kinds of goodies. We'd be stupid if we just stayed here a week."

So with the prospect of a idyllic summer spent fishing and loafing before them, they savored their meal of piping hot fish. The twilight faded into darkness.

"I'll get a lantern," Emerson offered, and walked into the bedroom.

Merrill relaxed in the rocking chair, gazing out the right-hand window at the lake. He heard a match being struck and light flared in the bedroom.

"Here we go," Emerson announced, returning with the lit lantern in his left hand. "There's another closet in there crammed with stuff."

"I think we should keep our mouths shut about this place," Merrill commented contentedly. "This cabin will be our little secret."

Emerson deposited the lantern on the kitchen counter, and the pale yellow glow illuminated the entire interior. "I agree."

"Maybe we could move in here permanently," Merrill recommended.

"It's too far out."

"How do we know that? There might be a town nearby where we can replenish our supplies now and then."

"If there was a town, someone would've discovered the cabin," Emerson said.

"You never know."

Emerson walked to the front door. "I need to take a leak. Be back in a jiffy."

"You'd better take your rifle," Merrill advised, pointing at the Beeman and the Remington. Both of their guns were leaning against the wall to the left of the entrance.

"I have my pistol," Emerson responded, and patted the Caspian on his left hip. He opened the door and stepped outside.

Feeling full and happy, Merrill lazily watched his friend pass the right-hand window. He swiveled his head to the right, expecting to see Emerson pass the side window on the west, but his companion didn't appear. Surmising that Emerson had stopped somewhere between the windows, probably at the corner, to take the leak, Merrill closed his eyes. His mind drifted, and he thought of the many childhood experiences he'd shared with Emerson.

Emerson?

Merill's eyes snapped open and he stared at the front door in confusion. He knew he'd dozed off, but for how long? A minute? An hour? He couldn't have been asleep very long because the front door was still ajar. "Emerson?"

A cool breeze blew into the room.

"Emerson?" Merrill called.

There was no reply.

Perplexed, Merrill rose and moved to the entrance. He poked his head outside, craning his neck to gaze at the bright stars dotting the firmament. "Emerson?"

Still no answer.

What the hell was going on? Merrill asked himself. He retrieved his Remington, ensured a round was in the chamber, and ventured outdoors. "Emerson? Where are you?"

The breeze rustled the trees in the forest behind the cabin.

Merrill walked to the southwest corner and scanned the terrain, his anxiety mounting. His chum would hardly have gone for a nighttime stroll. But if Emerson had been attacked, he would have managed to shout or fire a shot. So where could—

A tremendous commotion sounded from the direction of the lake, loud splashing punctuated by inarticulate, gasping cries. As quickly as the noise began, it abruptly ceased.

"Emerson?" Merrill yelled, and jogged toward the water. The night was moonless, and the surface gave the illusion of being a vast black pit. He listened for more splashing. Twelve feet from the lake he halted. "Emerson? Are you there?"

In the distance a wolf howled.

His body tensed. Merrill advanced to the edge of the water and surveyed the lake. A tingle ran down his spine. "Emerson! Answer me!"

A faint splash came from the water directly in front of him.

Merrill leaned forward, licking his lips, peering into the

night. Try as he might, he couldn't detect anything unusual. He resolved to return to the cabin and wait for daylight, and he was about to pivot and leave when a great, hulking form reared up out of the water and lunged. He felt bands of steel constrict around his arms, and he opened his mouth to scream as the creature surged backwards, bearing him into the lake. Water flooded down his throat, and he kicked and heaved in a vain attempt to break free. Panic seized him. And then something clamped on his neck, and he went oddly numb from his head to his toes. His lungs seemed to explode, and his mind shrieked a mental wail of despair.

Eternity claimed him.

CHAPTER ONE

The three women were standing near the base of the towering oak tree, conversing. Two of the three were blondes; the third had flowing black tresses.

"How'd you talk him into it?" asked the taller of the blondes. She was endowed with a slender figure, and her features were distinguished by a high forehead, prominent cheekbones, and thin lips. Her green eyes were matched by the color of her shirt, and brown pants and moccasins completed her attire. Around her slim waist was strapped a Smith and Wesson .357 Combat Magnum.

"Yeah, what did you do?" added the woman with the black hair. Her attractive countenance showed her Indian heritage. A buckskin dress, which she had designed and sewn together herself, accented her shapely build. Like the blonde, she wore moccasins.

"I didn't do anything special," responded the shorter blonde. She grinned, exposing her even white teeth, her rounded chin jutting downward. Her apparel consisted of a yellow blouse, blue pants, and brown leather shoes.

"Come on, Jenny. You can tell us," urged the tall blonde. "Cynthia and I are your best friends."

"That's right," Cynthia echoed, running her left hand through her dark hair.

"I know I can trust both of you," Jenny said, glancing from one to the other. She focused on the tall blonde. "Really, Sherry, I'm telling the truth."

"We know your husband better than that," Sherry responded.

Cynthia nodded. "And you know *our* husbands. So tell us how you did it so we can use the same tactic on them."

"Did you beg him?" Sherry inquired.

Jenny laughed lightly. "Of course not!"

"I'd never beg Geronimo for a thing," Cynthia stated. "He told me once that he married me because he considers me to be a strong-willed woman. If I begged him for something, he'd accuse me of being an imposter."

"I didn't beg Blade to go on a vacation," Jenny said.

"Then what *did* you do?" Sherry demanded. "Promise him extra whoopie?"

"Be serious," Jenny responded.

"I am. It works for me with Hickok," Sherry disclosed.

Jenny and Cynthia glanced at each other.

"You're kidding," Cynthia said.

"Nope," Sherry answered.

"You really promise Hickok more sex if he'll do what you want?" Jenny queried in disbelief.

"Well, I don't exactly promise him more sex," Sherry said. "I *give* him more sex."

"I don't follow you," Jenny remarked.

"Let's face facts. Most men are sex-starved maniacs," Sherry declared. "They can't get enough. And have you ever noticed how they always get romantic at the weirdest times?"

"Have I!" Cynthia interjected. "The other day I was doing the dishes and Geronimo came up behind me and started nibbling on my ear."

Sherry snickered. "Just like a man. What did you do?"

"I made him dry the dishes," Cynthia revealed.

All three enjoyed a hearty laugh.

"Anyway," Sherry went on when their mirth subsided, "if I want to wrap my hardheaded hunk around my little finger, all I have to do is give him more sex. We're accustomed to doing it on certain nights of the week when our work schedules don't conflict. With both of us being Warriors, one or the other has night duty every few days. And it's next to impossible to find time for lip locks when you have two kids running around the cabin."

"Lip locks?" Cynthia repeated quizzically.

"What do you call it?" Sherry rejoined.

"Making love," Cynthia said.

"In front of your son?" Sherry asked.

"No. We don't discuss sex in front of Cochise," Cynthia said. "He's only four, you know."

"Well, Ringo is almost five and Chastity is almost seven," Sherry stated. "They pick up on everything we say, so we use the term lip locks to discuss our plans for the evening in front of them without them being the wiser."

"Don't they get curious about what the expression means?" Jenny inquired. "Don't they ask you about it?"

"Sure. Now and then."

"And what do you say?" Jenny questioned.

"If they ask me, I tell them that I'll explain when they're older."

"And if they ask Hickok?" Cynthia queried.

"He always tells them it's a secret technique for summoning the stork."

"What stork?" Jenny wanted to know.

"The dummy keeps telling them that babies are delivered by storks," Sherry elaborated. "I'm going to have a heck of a time setting them straight when they're older."

"We're getting off the track," Jenny said. "You didn't finish your story about using sex to persuade Hickok to do what you want."

"It's simple. If I want something, and if I know he might

give me grief, I become romantic when he leasts expects it, when we have a spare moment. Afterwards, he's always a regular pussycat, and I can usually talk him into anything I want."

Jenny shook her head. "You're the last person I would have expected to use sex to get her way."

"Hey, I'm a Warrior, remember? I've been trained to employ psychological-warfare strategies," Sherry replied.

"But against your own husband?"

"Hickok is a man, and in the battle between the sexes a woman has to use every weapon she has," Sherry said.

Jenny frowned. "I don't think of sex as a weapon."

"Don't you ever use sex to influence Blade?" Sherry asked.

"Never," Jenny said.

Sherry glanced at Cynthia. "What about you?"

"The Sioux regard sex as a special, spiritual expression of love between the wife and husband. If I used sex as a weapon, I would betray the heritage of my people."

"Thanks heaps. The two of you are making me feel like a hussy."

Cynthia looked at Jenny. "So how did you persuade Blade to take this trip?"

"I used the same method women everywhere have used for ages. I nagged him to death."

"I don't like to nag," Sherry said. "It's too demeaning. I'd rather use sex to get what I want."

"Are you still planning to leave tomorrow?" Cynthia asked Jenny.

"Yep. Tomorrow morning. Which gives me about twenty-four hours to get all packed."

"Are you taking Gabe?" Sherry inquired.

"Yes."

"Hickok and I will baby-sit him if you want. He's the same age as Ringo and they're the best of buddies," Sherry said.

"Thanks, but no. Blade and I discussed whether to take Gabe along, and we decided we'd hurt his feelings if we left him behind," Jenny explained.

"You're missing a chance to have a second honeymoon," Sherry commented.

"Gabe is an integral part of our family. I know that many parents before the Big Blast viewed their children as hindrances to their careers, or as nuisances they couldn't wait to raise and boot out of the house. But the Elders have taught us better than that. We know children are a blessing bestowed on us by the Spirit so we can understand the Spirit's parental relationship to us by experiencing being parents ourselves," Jenny said.

Sherry sighed. "Sometimes I really wish I'd been born here at the Home instead of in Canada."

"You're part of the Family now," Jenny noted.

"Yeah. And I've been through the Warrior training courses. But I'll never know what it was like to be raised in the kind of environment where everyone sincerely tries to live the Golden Rule. Don't get me wrong. In the small town of Sundown where I was born, life was hard but relatively peaceful. We had to struggle just to keep food on the table. The people were generally nice, except for the usual scumbags. And, of course, we had the mutations to deal with," Sherry detailed.

"I know what you mean," Cynthia mentioned. "Since I was raised in the Dakota Territory, my background was similar to yours."

"You're both full-fledged Family members now," Jenny stressed. "It doesn't matter to the rest of us whether you were born at the Home or not. We love you just the way you are."

"Yeah. I know. It's funny. I never expected to wind up living in a Utopia," Sherry said. She gazed about her at the 30-acre compound constructed by a wealthy survivalist named Kurt Carpenter shortly before World War Three in northwestern Minnesota, near the former Lake Bronson State Park. Carpenter's foresight had ensured that his descendants, and those of the 30 people he had gathered together at the compound, would be able to hold their own in a world deranged by the ultimate insanity—devastating nuclear self-destruction. It was the idealistic Carpenter who had dubbed his retreat the Home and designated his loyal followers as his Family.

The man had built well, Sherry admitted to herself. To the west she could see the 20-foot-high brick wall that completely enclosed the compound on all four sides. At the inner base of the wall flowed the moat Carpenter had installed as another line of defense. A large stream entered the Home at the northwest corner, through an aqueduct, and was diverted to the south and the east along the bottom of the wall. At the southeast corner the two branches joined again and passed out of the Home through a second aqueduct. An enormous drawbridge situated in the middle of the west wall served as the entrance.

Carpenter's practical side was further demonstrated by his dividing the Home into sections. Almost the entire eastern half of the compound was preserved in its natural state or utilized for agricultural purposes. In the western portion were located six immense concrete bunkers, each devoted to a specialized use. And in the center of the Home, arranged in a line from north to south, were the cabins for the married couples. Sherry glanced over her left shoulder at Jenny and Blade's cabin, not 15 yards off, and thought of her own home, the next cabin to the south. Beyond hers was Cynthia's.

"So where is Blade taking you?" Cynthia asked Jenny.

"I don't know. He's keeping it as a big surprise. Apparently he got the idea from Plato."

"Did I hear someone mention my name?" asked a kindly voice to their rear.

They turned to find the Family's current Leader approaching at a leisurely stroll. His blue eyes seemed to twinkle with amusement as he regarded them. Long gray hair and a gray beard made him look older than his 50-odd years. A brown wool shirt and faded jeans clothed his lean frame. "How are you this morning, ladies?"

"We're fine," Jenny responded.

"Are you excited over your impending trip?" Plato asked.

"You know it."

"Where is Blade taking her?" Sherry inquired.

Plato chuckled as he reached them. "I'm not at liberty to divulge their destination. Blade requested that he be allowed to spring the surprise."

"Can't you give me a clue?" Jenny questioned eagerly.

Their wizened Leader reflected for a moment, then grinned. "Fair enough. You're aware, of course, that our Founder kept a journal of his activities and beliefs?"

"Certainly," Jenny said. "Carpenter's journal is kept in E Block, the library."

"Well, I was studying the journal several months ago when I came across an obscure reference to a two-week trip the Founder took. Intrigued, I checked through all of his material we have on file, and in a drawer containing copies of Carpenter's correspondence I found additional information."

"About what?" Jenny asked.

"Sorry. That's the only clue I can give you," Plato responded.

"You're a lot of help," Sherry muttered.

"I wouldn't want to spoil Blade's plans," Plato stated.

"Can you at least tell me if we'll be traveling very far so I know whether to pack a lot of extra clothes?" Jenny inquired.

"You're fishing, my dear," Plato said, and unexpectedly laughed.

Cynthia cleared her throat. "Will other couples be permitted to take trips to this mystery spot?"

"Perhaps," Plato answered.

"We should be allowed to go," Sherry declared. "Hickok and I could use a break, and so could Cynthia and Geronimo. For that matter, you'll probably need to keep a waiting list of those who want to go."

"Whether other couples are permitted to go will depend on what Blade and Jenny find when they arrive at their destination," Plato elaborated.

"You don't know what's there?" Jenny probed, taken aback by the revelation.

"If Carpenter's records are accurate, and if the ravages of

time haven't taken a severe toll, then I know," Plato said.

"You're not exactly brimming over with confidence," Sherry remarked.

Plato shrugged. "The best I can do is hope."

"It doesn't much matter," Jenny stated. "I'm so happy about going, I wouldn't care if Blade was taking us to a tar pit."

"How will you get there?" Cynthia brought up.

"We're taking the SEAL."

"Then you shouldn't have to worry about scavengers or mutations. The SEAL will make mincemeat out of any scuzzies who try to give you grief," Sherry mentioned.

"Scuzzies?" Plato repeated distastefully.

"Yeah. You know. Dirtballs. Lowlifes. Bloodsuckers."

"Are you referring to those misguided unfortunates who have succumbed to their own abysmal ignorance and who live by the admittedly brutal credo of might makes right?" Plato inquired.

"They're the ones. The scuzzies," Sherry said.

"Your husband has the rather quaint habit of alluding to them as cow chips," Plato noted.

"That's my hunk. He's as smart as a whip."

Plato idly glanced over Sherry's right shoulder and the corners of his mouth curled upward. "Are you making light of Hickok's powers of perception?"

"Didn't you hear me?" Sherry responding, raising her voice slightly. "I'm proud of my man. Hickok is as smart as they come. Of course, I'd never tell the lug to his face."

From behind them came a delighted cackle. "Too late, gorgeous. I heard that!"

CHAPTER TWO

A trio of newcomers, all men, joined the quartet.

"Oh, no!" Sherry declared, placing her hands on her cheeks, addressing the man on the right, a sinewy six-footer wearing buckskins and moccasins. Blond hair crowned his handsome features, and a blond mustache framed his mouth. In a holster on either hip rested a pearl-handled Colt Python revolver. "What are you doing here? I thought you were at the armory."

"Is that any way to greet your better half?" the gunman replied.

"As usual, Hickok, you've got it backwards," said the man on the left. The shortest of the three men, he possessed a stocky, powerful build. His clothing consisted of a shirt and pants fabricated from material that had once been part of a green canvas tent. Tucked under his belt next to his buckle was a genuine tomahawk, and under his right arm, snug in a shoulder holster, was an Arminius .357 Magnum. His features, like those of Cynthia, showed Indian ancestry.

"Who asked you?" the gunman retorted.

"Geronimo is right," stated the man in the middle, a giant

endowed with a herculean physique. Seven feet in height, his body rippled with layers of prodigious muscles scarcely contained by the black leather vest, green fatigue pants, and combat boots he wore. His hair was dark, his eyes were a striking gray. On each side of his waist, in a brown leather sheath, hung a big Bowie knife.

"And who asked you, Blade?" the gunman countered.

"Are you claiming to be the better half of our marriage?" Sherry demanded.

Hickok hooked his thumbs in his gunbelt and smirked. "I reckon I'd be plumb foolish to make such a claim, but I have it on good authority that I'm as smart as they come."

"See?" Sherry said, glancing at the others. "This is precisely the reason I didn't want him to hear me complimenting his brains. He'll walk around with a swelled head for a month!"

"Probably longer," Geronimo quipped.

"Not me," Hickok disagreed. "I'm the modest type."

"Right," Geronimo said sarcastically. "And so was George Armstrong Custer."

"Don't go pickin' on Custer," Hickok stated. "He would've won that scrape at the Little Big Horn if the weather had cooperated. That's why the Indians whipped Custer's tail."

"What are you babbling about? Custer, against orders, attacked an Indian encampment without bothering to verify the number of braves who would oppose him. He lost because he was stupid, not because of the weather," Geronimo said.

"Oh, yeah? I've read a few books on Custer, pard."

"So have I," Geronimo responded.

"Then you must have read about the haze," Hickok said.

"The what?"

"Custer rode to the crest of the hills overlooking the Little Big Horn and tried to spot the Indian camp through his field glasses, but there was too much haze," Hickok related. "Do you remember readin' about that?"

"Yeah, but—" Geronimo began.

"I rest my case," Hickok declared.

Plato smiled at Blade. "I can't imagine how you'll manage for a couple of weeks without your two compeers."

"I'll get by," Blade said, and grinned.

"Com-who?" Hickok asked, looking at Geronimo. "Were we just insulted?"

"The ladies have been pumping me for information concerning your trip," Plato mentioned.

"Oh?" Blade responded, his eyebrows arching as he gazed at his wife.

"We simply asked a few questions," Jenny said. "You can't blame us for being curious."

"Did you learn anything?" Blade queried.

"No," Jenny replied.

"I guess you'll just have to be patient and wait until we get there," Blade said.

"Why do women hate to be surprised?" Hickok wondered aloud.

"We do not," Sherry said.

"Bet me. Whenever I try to surprise you, you drive me nuts until you find out what the surprise is."

"No, I don't," Sherry insisted.

"Okay. Just remember you said that on your birthday."

"What are you planning to give me?" Sherry asked.

The gunman snickered. "I'm on a roll today."

Blade draped his right arm around Jenny's shoulders. "If you'll excuse us, we have preparations to make."

"Is that a hint?" Hickok inquired.

Sherry grabbed the gunfighter's right wrist. "Let's go. We have the cabin to ourselves until the kids get home from their schooling."

"What do you have in mind?" Hickok asked, and then an impish grin creased his face. "Oh." His blue eyes gleamed lecherously.

They walked off, heading to the south.

"Speaking of kids, where's Cochise?" Geronimo asked his wife.

"Spending the morning at Samson's," Cynthia disclosed.

"Cochise wanted to play with Benjamin, and Samson and Naomi offered to watch both boys until noon."

"Then we have *our* cabin to ourselves?" Geronimo asked.

"Yes. Why?"

Geronimo nodded at Blade, Jenny, and Plato. "We'll catch you later." He took hold of Cynthia's left arm. "Let's go."

"What's your rush?" Cynthia queried, then did a double take. "You mean right now?"

"I don't see any dishes in your hands."

Cynthia chuckled, gave a little wave, and they departed.

"Perhaps I should advise the midwives and Healers to be prepared for a busy spell nine months from now," Plato joked.

"Count us out," Jenny said. "We have too much packing to do."

"We could delay the start of our vacation for a day," Blade suggested to Jenny.

"Not on your life, buster. I've been after you for months to take time off from your job with the Freedom Force and your post as the head Warrior. You gave me your word that we can leave tomorrow morning, and I'm holding you to it."

"One more day wouldn't make a difference."

"It would to me," Jenny asserted.

Blade gazed tenderly at her for a moment, then sighed. "Okay. You're right. The vacation comes first. So why don't you begin packing and I'll check on the SEAL?"

"It's a deal," Jenny responded. She spun on her heels and hastened toward their cabin, humming softly.

Plato stepped up to Blade. "I haven't seen your wife this happy in years."

"Neither have I."

"You, however, don't seem to share her joy," Plato observed.

"I need to check on the SEAL," Blade reiterated, and started walking to the west.

"Mind if I accompany you?" Plato inquired, keeping pace with the giant.

"Suit yourself."

"What's bothering you?"

"Nothing," Blade said testily.

"I may not be an Empath, but I know when you are upset," Plato said. "If I'm prying, if I'm overstepping the bounds of our friendship, I'll desist. But I know you're troubled about something."

Blade glanced at the man who had been his mentor since the death of his father years before, his lips compressing. "I'm sorry, Plato. I shouldn't take out my frustrations on you."

"What frustrations, if I may ask?"

"The same ones I've been trying to deal with for almost a year and a half," Blade said. "The frustration of holding down two demanding jobs at the same time, when now I'm not wholly convinced one of the jobs is necessary. The frustration of having to constantly shuttle back and forth between Los Angeles and the Home, never spending more than a couple of weeks at either location. And the supreme frustration of struggling to deal with a wife who definitely doesn't want me on the Force, who wishes I would confine my activities to the Home and my post as the top Warrior."

"Perhaps if we examined each of your frustrations, we might resolve them," Plato recommended.

"Fat chance."

"Let's take a look at the first one," Plato said. "You say that you're not convinced one of your posts is necessary. May I assume you are referring to the Freedom Force?"

Blade nodded.

"But when the Force was first conceived, you believed the unit would be a critical component in enabling the Federation to deal with sundry threats," Plato reminded the Warrior.

"Yeah, I did, didn't I?" Blade replied, reflecting on that day in Los Angeles when the governor of the Free State of California had proposed forming a special strike squad, a team that would be prepared to fly out on a moment's notice to handle trouble spots as they arose. Was it *really* only 18 months ago?

Blade could recall the summit meeting as if it had taken place the day before. The leaders of the Freedom Federation, the league of seven organized factions dedicated to fostering the flickering embers of civilization in a country where barbarism reigned, had assembled in Anaheim, California, for a momentous meeting. The governor of California, one of the few states to retain its administrative integrity after the war, had been there. So had Plato. Also in attendance was the President of the Civilized Zone, the area in the Midwest including the former states of Wyoming, Colorado, Nebraska, Kansas, New Mexico, and Oklahoma, and part of Arizona and the northern portion of Texas. The U.S. government had evacuated hundreds of thousands of its citizens into this area during the war. Later, after the U.S. government collapsed and a dictator arose, the area was designated as the Civilized Zone.

Four other leaders were also at the meeting. The Flathead Indians, who now controlled Montana, sent the woman who presided over their tribal councils. The Cavalry, a group of superb horsemen who ruled the Dakota Territory, were represented by their top man. And the leaders of two other factions from Minnesota, the Clan and the Moles, were on hand to cast their votes on the creation of the Freedom Force.

Initially, Blade had favored the idea behind the force. An elite tactical unit, he reasoned, might help to neutralize the machinations of the Russians, who had wrested control of a section of the eastern United States during the war. And in addition to the Soviets, there were countless other menaces: scavengers, raiders, mutations, petty tyrants, despotic city-states, and more. In fact, there were too many menaces. Between his responsibilities as a Warrior and his duties on the Force, Blade seemed to spend all of his time away from his loved ones, confonting one danger after another. And most of the dangers, he had to admit, were encountered in his capacity as a Warrior.

Emotionally, though, his position with the Force had taken a harsher toll. In ten months of action he'd lost five of his team. Five! He blamed himself for each and every one. They'd died being true to their commitment to defend the Federation, but they had perished while under his command. Even as the thought entered Blade's mind, he heard Plato speak.

"Are you certain the Force isn't necessary, or are you endeavoring to justify your decision to disband the unit for a year?"

"My decision to disband the Force for a year stemmed from the problem my extended absences were causing at home. Jenny and Gabe were extremely upset. I needed the time to be with them, to stablize my family."

"And there was no other reason you disbanded the Force?"

"Like what?" Blade asked.

"Like perhaps the deaths of those five Force members affected you more than you have been willing to reveal. Perhaps the real motive was your desire to avoid losing any more personnel," Plato conjectured.

Blade looked at the Family Leader, impressed by Plato's insight. He shrugged. "Maybe it was a combination of the two."

"You were operating under a considerable strain," Plato suggested.

"That's the understatement of the decade."

"What will you do five months from now when the Federation leadership expects you to render a decision on whether or not you'll continue as the head of the Force?"

"I don't know."

"What does Jenny want you to tell them?"

"To go fly a kite."

They fell silent as they approached the vicinity of the six huge concrete blocks. The Founder had arranged the buildings in a triangular pattern, and each structure was known by a letter of the alphabet. At the southern tip was A Block, the Family armory, stocked with a variety of weapons. The Family Gunsmiths were responsible for ensuring the weapons were kept in perfect functional condition for the Warriors. One hundred yards northwest of the armory was B Block, the sleeping quarters for single Family members. The men were housed on the upper floor, the women on the lower. In a northwesterly line, again one hundred yards distant, stood C Block, the infirmary. Due east the same distance was D Block, which served as the Family's carpentry shop and all-purpose construction facility. One hundred yards farther to the east was E Block, the massive library Kurt Carpenter had personally stocked with almost five hundred thousand books. Family children were taught to read early, and nearly everyone at the Home read avidly. Finally, one hundred hards southwest of the library was F Block, the building utilized for storing their farming equipment and supplies, for preserving and preparing food, and for whatever other purposes the Tillers deemed appropriate.

Blade and Pluto angled toward the wide expanse between the blocks, the Family's primary area for socializing, where worship services were conducted, where the Elders held their open-air meetings, where the Musicians held their concerts, and where many of the older children congregated to play. Adults gathered there too, if they weren't working, to pass the time in pleasant conversation.

"So tell me again about this spot the Founder described as beautiful and restful," Blade prompted. He spied the vanlike SEAL parked in the middle of the open tract.

"I found a reference to the spot some years back, but the earlier reference was in error because it claimed the site was east of the Home. Actually, it's approximately ten miles to the northeast. The Founder described it as 'a small, beautiful lake undisturbed by the destructive hand of humankind,' a place where he could go to commune with the Spirit and sort out his thoughts," Plato detailed.

"And you're positive we won't need to take along sleeping bags and tents?" Blade queried.

"You shouldn't require them. The Founder had a cabin built near the north shore of this lake, a retreat he used frequently while the Home was under construction and before the war began. Logically, the cabin should still be there. In light of its remote location, I doubt the looting bands of scavengers have found the site. They tend to roam close to the cities and towns."

"We've been attacked by a few here," Blade noted.

"True. Then maybe you should take the tents and sleeping bags, just in case."

"I hope you're right about the lake and the cabin. Venturing into the Outlands is always a risky proposition, but the trip will be worth it if Jenny, Gabe, and I can forget all our cares and woes and have fun," Blade said.

Plato smiled. "Don't worry. You'll undoubtedly have the time of your lives."

CHAPTER THREE

"I saw something!" Jenny exclaimed, leaning forward in her seat to stare out the windshield.

"I saw it too," Blade said, and quickly applied the brakes. Twenty-five yards ahead and slightly to the left, at the edge of a stand of trees and dense underbrush, something had appeared for an instant. He'd glimpsed a brownish creature moving near a towering pine.

"What do you think it is?" Jenny asked.

"I don't know," Blade said.

"Maybe it's a mutation," Jenny noted.

From the seat behind them a childish voice piped up. "Can a mutant get in here, Dad?"

"No, Gabe," Blade answered. "The SEAL is virtually impervious."

"Im—what?" Gabe said.

"Impervious means the SEAL's body can't be penetrated by a bullet, cut by a knife, or smashed by a hammer," Blade explained.

"Wow! I wish my body was impervious," Gabe stated.

Carpenter's foresight served them in good stead. The Founder had spent millions of dollars to have the Solar Energized Amphibious or Land Recreational vehicle developed. Carpenter had realized his descendants would need a versatile, durable vehicle capable of negotiating the rugged postwar terrain, so he'd offered to foot the bill to have a prototype built. The automotive executives he'd approached had welcomed the opportunity to construct the ultimate all-terrain vehicle. They had viewed Carpenter as a strange eccentric who possessed enough money to indulge his fascination with ostentatious toys. Little did they suspect his true motive.

The automakers had performed their job well. The transport's green body was composed of a shatterproof and heat-resistant plastic fabricated according to Carpenter's rigorous specifications. As a security precaution, the shell was tinted to enable those within to see out while preventing anyone outside from observing the occupants. A set of puncture-resistant tires, each one two feet wide and four feet high, supported the vehicle.

Knowing that the war would drastically reduce the availability of fossil fuels, Carpenter had insisted that his "toy" be solar powered. Sunlight was collected by a pair of solar panels attached to the roof, and the energy was converted and stored in a bank of six revolutionary new batteries in a lead-lined casing underneath the SEAL. The experts had informed Carpenter that, if the solar panels weren't broken and the battery casing wasn't damaged, the transport would run forever.

"There! I saw it again!" Jenny said.

"What will you do if it's a mutant, Dad?" Gabe inquired.

"Blow the sucker to smithereens," Blade responded.

And well he could. After the automakers were done with their work, Carpenter had taken the SEAL to the Home and called in specialists, mercenaries who converted the seemingly innocuous transport into a four-wheeled arsenal. Four toggle switches on the dashboard controlled four armaments. The first toggle activated two 50-caliber machine guns mounted in recessed compartments directly under each front headlight. When the toggle was flicked, a small metal plate would slide upward and the guns would automatically fire. The second toggle launched the miniature surface-to-air missile mounted in the roof above the driver's seat, in front of the solar panels. Once the toggle was pressed, a panel in the roof moved aside and the heat-seeking missile shot into the sky toward its target. The third toggle was for the flamethrower hidden behind the front fender. At the proper moment, the driver worked the toggle and the fender lowered, the nozzle of the flamethrower would extend six inches, and anyone or anything in front of the SEAL would be fried to a crisp. For their last bit of handiwork, the mercenaries had included a concealed rocket launcher behind the grill.

"It's coming toward us!" Jenny declared.

Blade's brawny hands clasped the steering wheel tightly. Ever since one of the genetic deviates had killed his father he'd dreaded the sight of mutations. He glanced at the toggle switches, then at the trees, and abruptly laughed.

A mule deer, a four-point buck, stepped into the open and regarded the SEAL with curiosity. After several seconds it wheeled and bounded into the undergrowth.

"It was just a deer!" Gabe said, giggling.

Jenny frowned and leaned back in her seat. "I was that worried over a measly buck?"

"You'll have to relax more if you want to enjoy our vacation," Blade remarked.

"Weren't you concerned?" Jenny asked.

"Yeah," Blade admitted. "We both have to unwind, or we'll be seeing mutations and who knows what else behind every boulder and tree."

"I wasn't scared," Gabe declared.

"You weren't?" Jenny responded.

"Nope. Daddy will beat the crud out of any mutant that tries to hurt us," Gabe said.

Jenny gazed at Blade and grinned. "Yes. I bet he will."

"One day when I'm big like Daddy I'll have knives of my

own, and then I'll beat the crud out of those suckers," Gabe vowed.

"Where did you ever hear about beating the crud out of things?" Jenny inquired.

"From Ringo."

"Figures," Jenny said.

Blade chuckled and accelerated, glancing at both of his loved ones. The spacious interior of the SEAL afforded more than ample room. In the front there were two bucket seats with a console between them. Behind the bucket seats was a single seat running the width of the transport. The rear section was reserved for storing provisions. Under the storage area, in a recessed compartment, were tools and two spare tires. Jenny sat in the passenger-side bucket seat, while Gabe was sitting in the wide seat.

"How many miles have we traveled?" Jenny asked.

Blade consulted the odometer. "Seven miles."

"How far do we have to go?"

"That's my secret."

"You still won't tell me?"

"Nope."

"Turkey."

Blade smiled. "Hickok was right," he said, and surveyed the landscape in front of the transport. He was making a beeline to the northeast as Plato had advocated, driving overland, avoiding the denser tracts of vegetation. With its nearly indestructible body and enormous tires, the SEAL easily lived up to Kurt Carpenter's high expectations, traversing the rugged terrain effortlessly. Although the ride was bumpy, there were few obstacles the SEAL couldn't handle.

Patches of forest alternated with fields and low, rolling hills. Once they came to a steep ravine, and Blade skirted the eroded gorge rather than contend with the precipitous incline. Wildlife was abundant. Birds roosted in the trees or flew overhead. Rabbits darted from the path of the SEAL. Squirrels chittered at them. They saw other deer, and Jenny spotted a black bear on a nearby hill.

TERROR STRIKE 35

"Isn't it odd we haven't seen any mutants at all?" Jenny mentioned after they had covered eight and a half miles.

"There you go again," Blade said.

"I'm not being a worrywart," Jenny stated defensively. "But we know there are mutations out here."

"Yeah, Dad," Gabe interjected. "How come we haven't seen any?"

"To answer that, I'd have to explain about the three kinds of mutations," Blade replied.

"Go ahead. We have time to kill," Jenny prompted. "Gabe has to get the facts straight."

"What's the scoop, Dad?" Gabe added.

Blade bypassed a boulder half the size of the SEAL, and settled in his seat. "There are three kinds of mutations we know about, son. The first are those caused by the massive amounts of radiation unleashed during World War Three. Do you know what radiation is?"

"The yucky stuff that came from the missiles and the bombs?"

"Close enough. The radiation is responsible for animals born with two heads or six legs."

"Like the time those mutant wolves attacked the Tillers?"

"Exactly," Blade confirmed. "The second type of mutation is produced by the regenerating chemical clouds."

"The what?" Gabe queried.

"Do you know those green clouds that appear out of nowhere, floating low over the ground and swallowing people up?"

"Yep."

"They're the regenerating chemical clouds. They were used as a chemical-warfare weapon during the Big Blast, and they got out of control. They dissolve people, bones and all, but the clouds don't always dissolve animals because the agents in the clouds are specifically designed to leech onto the human metabolism."

"Huh?" Gabe said.

"The clouds don't swallow up all the animals. Many animals

are transformed into what we call mutates. They lose all their hair, their bodies become covered with pus-filled sores, and they try to eat every living thing they find," Blade detailed.

"They're gross," Gabe declared.

"The third kind of mutations are those genetically engineered by the scientists. Both before the war and afterward, there were scientists who created hybrids in test tubes, creatures that are half human and half something else. You name it, the scientists probably made it. Bear-men. Cat-men. Dog-men."

"Turtle-men?"

Blade smiled. "I don't know about turtle-men. I'll have to check on those."

"How about butterfly-men?"

"I don't think so."

"Or dinosaur-men?"

"We're getting off the track," Blade said. "We're supposed to be discussing why we haven't seen any mutants yet."

"Oh. Right."

"I doubt we'll see any of the genetically engineered mutations because they aren't that numerous," Blade said.

"Say, Dad?"

"Yes?"

"Are Lynx, Ferret, and Gremlin gene-ticklely engineered?" Gabe inquired.

"That's genetically engineered. And yes, they are," Blade said, thinking of the trio of mutants who were created by an insane scientist known as the Doktor to serve in his assassin corps, and who later defected to the Home and were now trusted Warriors.

"Will we see any mutates?" Gabe questioned.

"We could, so keep your eyes peeled at all times."

"And the other kind?"

"We might run into some of them. They're out there, but they're not lurking behind every tree, as I said before. The odds of bumping into one are about the same as those for bumping into a bobcat or a cougar."

TERROR STRIKE 37

"Uh-oh," Gabe said.

"What?" Blade responded, looking over his right shoulder.

"There," Gabe said, and pointed to the left.

Blade twisted in his seat, his eyes widening in surprise at the sight of a cougar 75 yards from the SEAL. The graceful feline, over six feet in length, was hurrying into a thicket, and it disappeared without a backward glance.

"I've seen pictures of cougars in books at the library," Gabe said. "That was a cougar, wasn't it?"

"Yes," Blade acknowledged.

"Then I bet we see a lot of mutants," Gabe stated.

"It was a fluke," Blade declared. "It doesn't mean we'll run into a lot of mutations."

"But you said we would if we saw a cougar."

"I said the odds were the same."

"Then we'll see mutants," Gabe insisted.

"Not necessarily," Blade remarked, hoping to allay any fears his son might have.

"Well, I hope we do," Gabe said.

"Why?" Jenny asked.

"Because I want to see Daddy blow the suckers to smithereens," Gabe answered.

Jenny laughed. "You're a chip off the old block."

"The what?"

"Never mind," Jenny told him.

Blade drove across a wide field, reflecting on the presence of the cougar. The big cats had been rare in Minnesota prior to the war, but afterwards, with the number of humans severely reduced and much of the cougars' range reverting to raw wilderness, they'd make a comeback.

"There's something I've been wondering about," Jenny commented.

"What?" Blade asked.

"A few years ago the countryside around the Home was crawling with those chemically spawned horrors, the mutates. But now there are hardly any. What happened?"

"We discovered the reason in the notes the Doktor kept. In an effort to destroy the Family, his assassin corps regularly released the green chemical clouds in the vicinity of the Home. Naturally, after the Doktor and his assassin corps were dealt with, the number of mutates dwindled."

"What about the clouds already unleashed?"

"We know the clouds are regenerating, but we don't know if the regeneration is sustained indefinitely. We suspect they have a limited life span," Blade replied, and his gaze drifted to the north. Immediately he tramped on the brake pedal.

"What's wrong?" Jenny asked, facing forward.

Rising above the trees, approximately a half-mile ahead, there reared a vertical column of smoke.

"A campfire, you think?" Jenny inquired nervously.

Blade nodded and drove in the direction of the smoke. "We must check it out."

"Why not go around? It's none of our business."

"I have to make it our business," Blade said.

"But why?"

"Because that campfire is about a mile from our destination," Blade divulged. "Whoever made the fire must still be there, and we need to learn if they're friendly or not."

"We're that close to our vacation spot?" Jenny queried in surprise.

"Yep."

"What will we do it they're raiders? Return to the Home?"

"If they're raiders, they'll regret being this close to the Home. We have our hearts set on this vacation, and I'm not going to allow anyone or anything to stand in our way."

"Go get 'em, Dad," Gabe stated.

The SEAL entered a stretch of woods, and Blade reduced speed to five miles an hour, skillfully weaving the transport among the trunks. His window was down, and he leaned to the left, listening for alien sounds, for voices, laughter, or any noises indicating the presence of another party. "Get the Commando," he directed.

Jenny climbed from her seat, over the console, and knelt next to Gabe so she could reach into the storage section.

The woods thinned and Blade pressed on the accelerator,

pushing the speedometer to 20. He focused on the spiraling plume of smoke, gauging the distance. He didn't want to blunder into the camp of whoever made the fire. The SEAL's air-cooled and self-lubricating engine produced a muted whine, instead of the raspy gowl so prevalent in prewar vehicles, and he doubted the SEAL could be heard more than 30 yards away. With luck, he might be able to catch the fire-makers off guard.

Jenny returned to her seat, laden with weapons. In her hands she held one of Blade's favorite autoloaders, a Commando Arms Carbine. Converted to full automatic capability by the Family Gunsmiths and fitted with a 90-shot magazine of .45-caliber ammunition, the Commando, which Blade found reminiscent of the ancient Thompson submachine guns, was a devastating piece of firepower. Over Jenny's left shoulder was slung a Beretta BM 62 auto-rifle, and in a holster on her right hip a Ruger Super Blackhawk .44 Magnum, a powerful handgun she had to hold with both hands to fire accurately, a gun she had practiced with many times.

"Hey, don't I get a gun?" Gabe asked, leaning on the console.

"No, you don't," Jenny said.

"Why not? Daddy has taught me how to shoot."

"I know. But there might be danger up ahead."

"That's why I want the gun," Gabe noted with childish simplicity.

"Not now," Blade interjected. "Sit back in your seat and keep quiet."

"But I want to help. I want to blow some of the suckers to smithereens," Gabe offered.

"First of all, we don't know if we'll be blowing anyone to smithereens," Jenny said. "Second, you're too young to be shooting people."

"How old do you have to be, Mom?"

"Be quiet, Gabe," Blade ordered. "I won't say it again."

Gabe made a hissing noise and sat back in his seat.

"Thank you," Jenny said.

Gabe crossed his arms on his chest and pouted.

Blade drove forward, watching the smoke. He slowed when he estimated he was within 100 yards of the campfire, and the SEAL crawled another 50 yards before he applied the brakes. "You stay here with Gabe," he told his wife. "I'm going to go have a look."

"Nothing doing. Where you go, I go."

"And leave Gabe here by himself?"

Jenny gazed to the north. "Why risk exposing yourself? Why don't we drive right up to the campfire in the SEAL? There hasn't been a bullet made that can penetrate the SEAL's synthetic shell. You said so yourself."

"Bullets, no. But a hand grenade or a bazooka could damage the transport extensively. If they're raiders, there's no predicting the type of weaponry they might have."

"I don't like you leaving us."

"It can't be helped," Blade said.

Jenny frowned. "I'll give you two minutes. Then I'm coming to get you."

"You'll stay put."

"You're my husband. Don't be ridiculous."

"All right," Blade said. "But give me fifteen minutes."

"Here," Jenny stated, extending the Commando. She glanced at the steering wheel. "Too bad you've never given me driving lessons."

"I will the first chance I get," Blade promised, taking the carbine and opening his door. "I won't be long." He dropped to the ground and took a moment to double-check the magazine.

Jenny and Gabe materialized at the window.

"Be careful, Daddy."

"I will, son."

"Fifteen minutes," Jenny said.

"Close the windows and lock the doors," Blade instructed her. "If anyone or anything tries to get in, lean on the horn."

"I'll blow 'em to smithereens!" Gabe declared.

"Enough, already, with the smithereens," Jenny said. Her

eyes locked on her husband, silently expressing the depth of her affection. "Take care."

"You know it," Blade replied, and jogged toward the smoke.

CHAPTER FOUR

Blade advanced warily, moving bent over at the waist, scrutinizing the undergrowth carefully. There were fewer and fewer trees the farther he went. When he reached a point approximately 20 yards from the smoke, he heard a peal of laughter. Someone was having a good time. He cocked his head and detected the murmur of conversation.

There was definitely more than one person.

He stalked through the waist-high weeds, the Commando at the ready, pausing between each step to listen. Twenty more yards were covered, and then he saw the flickering flames of the campfire. Dropping to his elbows and knees, he continued to narrow the range. The voices became louder, and after a bit he could distinguish individual words. In another 15 yards he could hear them clearly, and he flattened and crawled to within eight yards of the speakers.

"—waste of our damn time!"

"We'll find the place yet."

"Like hell we will!"

By cautiously parting the weeds with the Commando barrel,

Blade could see the fire and the eight people seated around it. Five were men, three were women. All wore filthy clothes. Their hair was unkempt, and all bore smudge marks on their faces. Their clothing consisted of a mix of tattered jeans, torn shirts, and old leather garments.

"We'll find it!" declared a man with a bushy brown beard and brown eyes. "We know it's in this area somewhere."

"But where?" snapped a weasel of a man whose oily black hair was plastered to his head. "It's like looking for a needle in a haystack!" He wore jeans, a tan shirt, and a black leather jacket.

"Lighten up, Roy," said a young redheaded woman. Her tight-fitting clothes, a blue blouse and jeans, seemed to have been molded to her shapely contours. "One minute we're shooting the breeze, and all the vibes are mellow, and the next you're griping and whining and spoiling the whole mood."

"I don't whine, you bimbo," Roy retorted angrily.

"Don't call Tammy a bimbo," the man with the beard warned. "I don't like to have my wife insulted."

"No offense meant, Jared," Roy said, but his contemptuous tone belied his statement.

"I know we're in the right area," Jared said. "And just think of what it will be like if we find this place! We'll never go hungry again. We'll never have to scrounge for food."

What place were they talking about? Blade wondered. He could see they were well-armed. Each person carried a rifle slung over a shoulder and a handgun in a hip holster.

"They have weapons there, an entire armory we can use," Jarad went on. "I heard tell they even have a library with thousands of books—"

"Who the hell cares about books?" Roy sneered.

A library! An armory! Blade's eyes narrowed.

"Those of us who can read care about books," Jared said. "Trust us, Roy. All we have to do is find the Home and we're set for life."

They were raiders planning to attack the Home! Anger washed over Blade, a sense of outrage at the thought of the harm the band could inflict on the Family, and heedless of his personal safety, he stood and strode toward the camp, the Commando level at his waist.

A brunette was the first to notice the enraged giant coming through the weeds. "Look out!" she cried, and leaped to her feet, her left hand going for her revolver.

"Don't even think of it!" Blade barked, stepping into the clear, swinging the Commando from side to side, waiting for one of them to grab a gun. He hoped they would give him an excuse to finish them right there.

Eight faces gaped in astonishment at the Warrior.

"Who the hell are you?" Roy demanded.

"Someone who was in the right spot at the right time," Blade said cryptically.

"We don't know you, mister," Jared stated, "and we don't want any trouble."

"You've got it, in spades," Blade declared.

"What did we ever do to you?" Tammy asked.

"It's what you were planning to do to those I'm sworn to protect that matters," Blade responded.

"What are you talking about?" Jared queried nervously.

"Don't play innocent with me. I overheard you discussing the Home. I know you plan to try and raid our compound."

"Your compound?" Jared said, and glanced at his companions in bewilderment.

Blade took a pace nearer and trained the Commando on the man named Jared, and as he did a hard object jammed him in the small of the back and a flinty voice spoke from right behind him.

"Let go of the hardware or you're dead!"

"Okay!" Blade deliberately blurted out, allowing his shoulders to droop dejectedly, and he made a motion as if he were tossing the carbine to the grass. Instead, he pivoted, spinning in a tight arc even as he sidestepped to the left, and he brought the Commando around and up.

A hefty man in a leather jacket, brown shirt, and jeans was just beginning to react when the stock of the Commando slammed into his arms, deflecting his Marlin 336 CS aside. An instant later the Commando's barrel struck him in the temple and he staggered backward and slumped to his knees. The Marlin slipped from his fingers.

The rest of the men and women were rising.

Blade rotated, covering the band, standing sideways so he could keep an eye on the one he'd slugged. "Put your hands up!" he commanded.

"You don't understand!" Jared declared, and took a step toward the Warrior.

Blade pointed the Commando at the bearded man, his finger tightening on the trigger.

"We don't want to hurt you!" Jared said, extending his arms with the palms out. "Really!"

"Sure," Blade replied sarcastically, his finger easing off the trigger.

"You misunderstood," Jared asserted. "We don't plan to attack the Home. We've heard wonderful things about the Home, and we came all this way to see if we could *live* there."

Amazement replaced Blade's anger, and he looked at each of them, stunned to behold evident sincerity on every countenance. "You what?"

"We've traveled hundreds of miles in the hope of being allowed to live at the Home," Jared said.

"Explain yourself," Blade directed, still suspicious of a trick.

Jared gestured at the others. "We were in Grand Rapids when we first heard about the Home. Grand Rapids, Minnesota, that is. Have you ever been there?"

"No," Blade admitted while continually scanning the band for a hint of treachery.

"It's a small town east of the Chippewa National Forest. About seven hundred people live there, making their living by fishing and hunting and trading. We were at a bar when we heard an old trapper talking to some men concerning the time he was captured by the inhabitants of an underground city in the north-central part of the state. He was out exploring, trying to find prime game areas for trapping, when he was caught by these people called the Moles. Do you know who they are?"

Blade nodded. Indeed he did. He had had many dealings with the Moles in their capacity as an ally of the Family in the Federation.

"These Moles told the trapper to stay away from that region. They apparently aren't too fond of strangers and don't permit anyone near their underground city."

Blade pursed his lips. Everything Jared had said so far rang true. The Moles' underground city had initially been a series of hasty fallout shelters dug by a man named Carter and some others shortly before the outbreak of the war. Certain that the war was imminent and doubting they had the time to construct a suitable retreat, Carter and company had driven far from civilization and hiked into the Red Lake Wildlife Management Area. Once there they'd simply started digging. They survived the war, and their descendants had expanded on the original shelters, adding on a network of tunnels and chambers. On the ground, over the heart of their complex, they had built a massive mountain of clay as added protection and insulation. Eventually their city had become known as the Mound.

"They released the trapper and sent him packing," Jared was saying. "While he was there they told him about their allies in something called the Freedom Federation. One of the allies they mentioned was the Family."

Blade relaxed slightly. He was beginning to believe Jared, and he was gratified to learn the Moles were not indulging in their old practice of slaying or enslaving every stranger they encountered. Or were they? "Wait a minute," he interrupted. "How long ago was the trapper caught?"

"Not quite two years ago," Jared said. "Why?"

"No reason. Continue."

"Excuse me," Tammy spoke up.

"What is it?" Blade asked.

"Can I take care of Harold?" she inquired, and pointed at the hefty man still on his knees, blood trickling from a gash in his temple, his eyes open but unfocused. "He was on guard duty, and he must not have seen you sneak in."

"Go ahead," Blade said. "But keep your hands where I can see them."

The woman walked to the guard and knelt beside him. She started inspecting the wound. "Harold? Are you all right?"

"Is it night?" Harold asked, swaying unsteadily.

"No?"

"Then why am I seeing stars?"

Tammy went to reach into the right back pocket on her jeans.

"Not so fast!" Blade warned. "Use two fingers."

Tammy froze, staring at the Commando, and slowly removed a red bandanna from the pocket. "This is all I wanted," she explained, and used the bandanna to dab at the blood.

"Go on with your story," Blade told Jared.

"Well, the information we learned about the Family fascinated us. The trapper talked about the Home, about the library and the huge armory and a tall wall that keeps out all the wild animals and the mutants. But what interested us the most was the news that married couples live at the Home in peace and security. Their children are educated and raised in relative safety."

Blade's mouth curved downward. He didn't like the idea of the Moles relating so much information about the Family, particularly not the fact that the armory existed. Weapons were valued at a premium in the Outlands, and any large band of raiders might be tempted to try and destroy the Family simply for the sake of acquiring an immense arsenal. "You seem to attach a lot of importance to the security and safety the Home and the Family have to offer," he commented.

"All of us were born in the Outlands. We've spent our entire lives living by our wits, barely surviving at times. No one is safe in the Outlands, mister. You must know that."

"I do," Blade said. The Outlands was the designation for any and all territory outside recognized jurisdictions, and included a major portion of the country. With the collapse of civilization, most of the U.S. had reverted to a barbaric level and survival of the fittest was the law of the land. Life in the Outlands, as the staying went, was cheap. People could be shot without provocation, or have their throats slit in the middle of the night. Killings, robbery, rape, and worse were commonplace. Blade had ventured into the Outlands a number of times, and on each occasion he had barely escaped with his life.

"Then you know why we want to find the Home, why we want to live there," Jared stated, and nodded at Tammy. "She and I want to have kids. We want to see them grow up healthy and strong. Most of all, we want to see them grow up, period. The Outlands is no place to try and raise a family."

"You have a point," Blade conceded.

"What's your name?" Jared asked.

"Blade."

"I'm Jared." He pointed at Tammy. "That's my wife, Tammy. Harold is the one you clobbered." He indicated the weasely man. "That's Roy. He joined us in Bemidji."

"Howdy," Roy said.

Blade said nothing, his gray eyes regarding the man coldly. He instinctively distrusted the weasel.

Jared pointed at each of the others. "That's Lloyd, with the torn T-shirt, and the brunette is his wife, Betty. The guy with the Winchester is Jim, and the woman next to him is Alice, his squeeze. The guy wearing the jeans with the holes in the knees is Tom."

Each person offered a friendly greeting.

"Hello," the Warrior said when the introductions were completed.

"And you're really from the Home?" Jared queried.

"I don't make it a habit to lie."

"Will you take us there?" Tammy asked hopefully.

"Not so fast," Blade replied. "Did all of you live in Grand Rapids?"

"None of us did. We were just passing through," Jared said.

"You wandered around a lot?"

"All over."

"And how did you feed yourselves?"

Jared blinked a few times and looked at his wife before answering. "Oh, we did odd jobs for food. Or we scrounged if we had to."

Blade scrutinized the group. "In other words, you're scavengers."

"You could call us that," Jared conceded reluctantly. "But we're not like most scavengers."

"Oh?"

"No. We don't go around killing people for the fun of it. We don't steal and loot. We try to live our lives honestly."

Blade studied Jared's features, measuring the man's integrity. "I've never heard of honest scavengers before."

"You must believe me! We're not murderers. The only times we've killed were when we were attacked, in self-defense. Why do you think we can't stand living in the Outlands any longer? Because we're sick and tired of all the senseless killing. We're sick and tired of always having to be on the alert for danger. And some of us want to have children. Could you imagine raising a kid under such conditions?" Jared inquired passionately.

The Warrior glanced at Tammy and Harold. She was assisting him to his feet. "No, I wouldn't like to rear a family in the Outlands."

"Then tell us. Do you think we have a chance to be admitted to the Home?"

"I don't know," Blade replied, facing Jared. "The decision isn't mine to make. Whether you're permitted to live there is for the Elders to decide."

"Who are the Elders?"

"Our Elders decide policy issues, and their decisions are implemented by our Leader."

"Will they let us live there?" Jared asked.

"I really don't know. Our compound can only handle so many people, and we already have about a hundred living there."

Jared frowned and his shoulders slumped. "We didn't know."

"You still might be granted permission," Blade said encouragingly. "And even if the Elders deny your petition, you might be allowed to live at Halma with the Clan."

"The who?"

"Another of our allies. The Clan were refugees from the Twin Cities, and the Family helped relocate them in Halma, a small town west of the Home," Blade explained.

"Do you—" Jared began, then stopped, staring past the Warrior, his eyes widening.

Blade turned.

Coming through the weeds were Jenny and Gabe. She had the Beretta pressed to her right shoulder. Gabe walked behind her, his head craned to the right so he could see the scavengers.

"These are my wife and son," Blade introduced them. "Jenny and Gabe."

"This is just great!" Jenny stated as she moved to Blade's left side. "Here I was, fearing for your life, and I find you socializing." She lowered the rifle.

"Who are these people, Dad?" Gabe wanted to know.

"Don't worry," the Warrior said. "They won't hurt us." He looked at the band.

Jared's right hand streaked to his revolver, a Smith and Wesson Model 65, and the handgun swept up and out, the barrel aimed at Blade and his loved ones.

CHAPTER FIVE

Blade swung into action the moment he saw Jared's hand sweep toward the holster. He lunged to his left, his huge arm encircling Jenny and Gabe, bearing them to the ground with his body in front of theirs, shielding them from the anticipated shot. Expecting to feel a searing pain as the slug tore through him, he twisted as he went down, training the Commando on the scavengers. He could see Jared sighting the Smith and Wesson, apparently intent on making an accurate shot, but the revolver wasn't aiming at Blade, Jenny, or Gabe.

The scavenger was pointing the gun at something behind them.

A snarling form hurdled over the Warrior and his family, springing at the scavengers. The Smith and Wesson boomed, but the shot missed. Before Jared could fire again, a feral feline landed on all fours, uttered a piercing, raspy scream of rage, and launched itself at the man named Harold.

For the space of a second, as the creature had alighted and girded its leg muscles to execute the leap at Harold, Blade glimpsed the thing clearly. Goose bumps broke out on his skin.

He recognized their attacker immediately. The characteristics were unmistakable; there was the hairless body covered with blistering sores oozing sickly yellowish pus, the otherwise dry, cracked, peeling skin, the two mounds of green mucus in place of ears, and the overpowering stench associated with animals caught in the green chemical clouds and transformed into ravenous horrors.

The thing was a mutated bobcat!

Harold screamed as the 60-pound fury pounced on his chest, its front claws slashing at his face and neck, its rear claws digging deep into his flesh. He staggered backwards, flailing at the mutate to no avail.

Jared tried to get a bead on the mutate, but couldn't shoot for fear of hitting Harold.

Blade shoved himself erect and closed in, gripping the barrel of the Commando and swinging the machine gun as if it were a club. The stock smashed into the mutate and dislodged the beast, sending it tumbling to the ground, where the creature promptly regained its footing and growled at the Warrior.

"Look out, Dad!" Gabe yelled.

The mutate vaulted at Blade's midriff, its claws extended to rake his stomach.

Blade whipped the Commando in a vicious swipe, catching the feline on the head and knocking it to the grass a second time. As it rolled and rose to its feet, Blade reversed his grip on the Commando, and was about to cut loose when he realized Tammy stood a few yards behind the bobcat, in his line of fire. Instead, he released the Carbine and drew his Bowies, meeting the mutate's next rush head-on.

With its mouth wide open, exposing its tapered fangs, the bobcat took two bounds and leaped.

The Warrior twisted his torso, evading those razor claws, and buried his left Bowie in the mutate's neck, sinking the blade to the hilt and impaling the bobcat in midair. The mutate went limp, but Blade still brought the right Bowie around and down, driving the point of the knife into the creature's skull.

Blood spurted from the mutate's nostrils and a putrid bile

spewed from its mouth. Unexpectedly, the bobcat came to life again, convulsing violently, its legs kicking wildly, and then it sagged, suspended by the knives, lifeless.

Blade placed the body on the ground, pressed his right boot onto the mutate's spine, and wrenched the Bowies out. Both knives dripped blood and pus. He heard a cough and looked to his right.

Harold lay flat on his back, his face severely lacerated, his throat literally torn to ribbons. His hands were clasped to his neck, and crimson spilled over his fingers and sprayed in all directions. He gasped and groaned, his mouth opening and closing, sheer terror reflected in his eyes.

"Are you okay?" Jenny asked Blade, standing and lending a hand to Gabe so he could rise. "I don't see any scratches. Did the mutate nick you?"

"No," Blade said, squatting. He wiped the Bowies clean on the grass and slid them into their sheaths. "I'm fine."

The band of scavengers gathered around Harold. Jared leaned over their companion. "Do you want us to try and get word to your mother and brother?"

Harold didn't respond. His lips quivered, his eyelids fluttered, and he expelled a protracted breath.

"That poor man," Jenny commented sadly. "Is there anything we can do?"

Blade shook his head. In addition to the deep cuts and slashes, splotches of pus were visible intermixed with the blood on Harold's neck, and mutate pus was as toxic as the deadliest of known poisons. Once the pus entered the human bloodstream, the affected individual seldom lasted more than a few days.

There were tears in Tammy's eyes when she bent down and kissed the doomed man lightly on the forehead. "We're so sorry, Harold. You're one of our best friends. I wish there was something we could do for you."

Harold suddenly arched his back, his arms dropped to his sides, and he stiffened and expired.

"Harold!" Tammy cried.

"It's no use," Jared said, feeling Harold's left wrist for a pulse. "He's gone."

Blade stared at the scavengers, noting their expressions of legitimate sorrow. All except for one. The weasel, Roy, was staring at Jenny.

Jared glanced up at the Warrior. "I'm sorry if I startled you. I saw the thing coming at you and there wasn't time to give any warning." He paused. "I thought I could nail the damn mutation before it got to us."

"You tried," Blade said.

"Not hard enough."

The scavenger wearing the torn T-shirt cleared his throat. "We should bury Harold. He's been with us for years, and I'm not about to let the buzzards or any other animals get to him."

"We'll bury him," Jared assured him.

Jenny leaned closer to her husband. "Who are these people, anyway?" she whispered.

Blade made the introductions, leaving the weasel for last. "And this one is Roy," he concluded gruffly.

"Hello," Jenny said.

"Hello, yourself, beautiful," Roy responded, smirking. "So you're the big lug's wife, huh? I can't imagine what you see in him. If you—"

Before Roy could continue, Blade was on him. He grabbed the scavenger by the front of the tan shirt and lifted, his enormous shoulder and arm muscles bulging, hoisting Roy overhead. A flaming scarlet tinged the Warrior's cheeks.

Transfixed by the abrupt assault, the other scavengers gaped.

"Let me go!" Roy demanded angrily, pounding his fists on the giant's forearms.

"Gladly," Blade responded, and hurled the weasel at the ground.

Roy hit hard on his left side and rolled several yards. He rose unsteadily to his knees, striving to unsling his rifle, but the tip of a combat boot rammed into his abdomen, doubling him over in agony.

Blade drew back his right foot to kick the scavenger again.

"Blade! Please! Don't!" Jenny interceded.

The Warrior stopped, his foot ready to lash out, and looked at her.

"He's not worth it," Jenny said.

"I should break every bone in his body," Blade stated harshly.

"Why stoop to his level? No harm has been done."

Blade hesitated, his fists clenching and unclenching. He saw Gabe watching in rapt fascination, and he thought of the example he was setting for his son. He wanted to beat the weasel to a pulp, but what effect would the sight have on Gabe?

"You bastard!" Roy fumed, shoving to his knees again. "I'll get you for this!"

Blade reached down and clamped his right hand on the scavenger's throat. He pulled Roy to a standing posture and glared into the man's defiant eyes. "Don't push me."

Roy tried to pry the Warrior's fingers fron his neck, but the steely vise only constricted tighter.

"This is the first and only warning you'll receive," Blade stated flatly. "I won't tolerate anyone treating my wife with disrespect. And no one—absolutely *no one*—comes on to my wife more than once. If you make the same mistake again, you'll answer to me. Do you understand?"

The scavenger merely glowered.

"You're a stubborn little turd, aren't you?" Blade remarked, and shook Roy until the weasel's teeth chattered. "What's it going to be? Are you going to behave yourself?"

"Yeah," Roy hissed, and sneered contemptuously.

"Why don't I believe you?"

"I won't try and put the make on your wife!" Roy snapped. "What else do you want me to say?"

"Not a word," Blade replied, and released his grip.

The scavenger toppled to the grass. He sat up and rubbed his sore neck.

Jared stepped over to the Warrior. "I'm sorry about this. He's been this way ever since we met him."

"Why'd you let him hook up with you?" Blade asked, his flinty gaze on the weasel.

Jared shrugged. "We can always use another gun. To his credit, he always did his share of the work."

"I can tell you here and now that he won't be permitted to live at the Home, and I doubt the Clan will accept him either. The rest of you can still apply to the Elders, but he might as well return to whatever hole he crawled out of," Blade said.

"You won't hold his actions against us?"

"You're not to blame for his behavior."

Jared breathed a sigh of relief. "Thanks. Will you take us to the Home as soon as we're done burying Harold?"

"No."

"No?" Jared repeated, perplexed. "Why not?"

"We're on a special trip, a vacation, the first I've taken away from all my duties in years. I'm not about to let anything interfere with it. I'm sorry."

Tammy joined them. "Are you sure you're not holding Roy's conduct against the rest of us?"

"I give you my word I'll take you to the Home after our vacation is over," Blade promised.

"How long will that be?" Tammy queried.

"About two weeks."

"Two weeks!" Jared exclaimed. "But we've come so far."

"Which is why another two weeks won't make much of a difference," Tammy said, taking his hand and squeezing reassuringly.

Jared glanced at her, then at the giant. "I guess we don't have any choice."

"Blade, we could take the time out to return to the Home," Jenny proposed.

"And what if a new threat has arisen? What if the Elders want to send me on another run, or the leaders of the Freedom Federation require my services again?"

"We've only been gone half a day," Jenny said.

Blade stared at her. "Do you want to take the risk of spoiling our trip?"

TERROR STRIKE

Her forehead creased as she pondered the question. "No," she finally admitted. "I don't."

"Then we continue to our destination," Blade said, and faced the head of the band. "Can you survive out here for two weeks?"

Jared nodded. "No problem. We'll hunt game for our food, and we know how to make sturdy shelters. We'll be okay."

"Then I'll swing by on our return trip and pick you up. We can cram most of you into our transport and the rest can sit on the roof. What do you say?"

"We'll be counting the minutes," Jared said, and smiled.

The Warrior offered his right hand. "Until then."

Smiling broadly at the prospect of achieving their goal, Jared shook vigorously.

Blade nodded at the others, but purposely ignored the weasel, and departed with Jenny and Gabe, making for the SEAL.

"Take care!" Jared called after them. "Don't let anything happen to you!"

"We'll be back," Blade pledged, and waved.

With hopeful expectation on their faces, the scavengers watched until the trio were no longer visible.

"I can't believe it!" Lloyd declared. "Our dreams have come true!"

Jared pivoted and gazed at Roy. "No thanks to you. I want you to leave. Now."

His lips compressing in resentment, Roy stood. "And what if I don't want to go?" he demanded. He saw Lloyd, Tom, and Jim close in on him and suddenly found himself surrounded.

"You don't have any choice," Jared said. "We've tolerated your attitude for as long as we can. Lloyd, Jim, and I have all seen you looking at our wives. But you were never blatant about it, so we let your conduct pass. This Blade has made us realize we've been fools. I can safely say I speak for the rest when I tell you to take a hike. And don't ever come back."

Roy glared at each of the men. "Just like that?"

"Just like that," Jared said.

"After all we've been through?"

"Don't play on our sympathy. We don't have any for a man who lusts after every woman he meets. Just leave, Roy, before we're tempted to hurry you along."

Roy glanced at the women, and the loathing he perceived on their countenances added to his simmering fury. "Fine! Be that way! I'll leave. And all you can go to hell."

"If I were you, I wouldn't head south," Jared advised. "That's the way Blade went, and I doubt you want to bump into him again." He stepped aside and motioned with his right arm. "Don't try to sneak back and cause us any trouble. We'll kill you if you do."

"Bastards!" Roy fumed, and walked away from them to the east. "I hope the mutants get the bunch of you!" He stormed into a stand of trees, his blood boiling, tempted to take a few shots at his former comrades. But he knew Jared was a man of his word, and he didn't like the odds. For 50 yards he tramped through the brush until his rage began to abate. He remembered the mutate, and quickly unslung his Ruger Model 77R.

There was no sense in being careless.

He absently gazed at the sky, thinking of the giant, and hatred welled within him. This was all the giant's fault! He told himself. He'd only hooked up with the lousy band because he planned to eventually get into Tammy's pants, with or without her consent, and now the damn giant had ruined his scheme. Months of biding his time and waiting for Tammy and him to be left alone, and it was all for nothing!

Damn!

Damn!

Damn!

Several minutes elapsed, and he stalked onward until he heard an odd whine. He was almost to the edge of a field, and he crouched, gazing to the southeast in the direction of the noise. Seconds later a large green van came into view, driving slowly to the northeast. The driver's window was down, and Roy blinked in surprise when he recognized the man behind the wheel.

The rotten giant!

He watched intently as the vehicle cruised across the field and vanished over a low hill. Then he rose and walked to where the van's immense tires had flattened the vegetation and left rutted impressions in the soil. Where were they headed? he wondered. The giant had mentioned taking a vacation. But to where? Probably not very far, if the bastard intended to return within two weeks and pick up Jared and the others.

Roy glanced at the low hill, wishing he could avenge himself on the man he hated most in the world. An idea occurred to him, and a crooked grin twisted his visage. The van wasn't moving very fast, and the vehicle was leaving a trail any idiot could follow. Shadowing them would be easy. And if he stayed on their tracks, sooner or later they would stop to enjoy their vacation. They'd undoubtedly be engrossed in their fun and off their guard. The very last person they would expect to see would be him.

He snickered.

Yes, sir! This must be his lucky day! He could take his revenge on the son of a bitch, and then have his way with the prick's foxy momma. The thought of kissing her lovely body made him salivate, and Roy cackled as he changed direction and hastened to the northeast.

CHAPTER SIX

"Is this your surprise spot?"

"Yep."

"Oh, Blade! It's lovely!" Jenny declared happily.

"What do you think, Gabe?" Blade asked, shifting in his seat and looking at his son.

"Can we fish in the lake?"

"You bet."

"Will we live in a tent like we do when we camp out in the Home?" Gabe inquired.

"No. We'll be staying in a cabin."

"What cabin, Dad?"

Blade turned and nodded at the log structure on the north side of the lake. He had braked the SEAL next to the western shore, 500 yards from Kurt Carpenter's retreat. "That cabin."

"Does anyone live there?" Gabe questioned.

"Nope."

"Then why is the door open?"

Blade's eyes narrowed and he leaned over the steering wheel. To his consternation, the cabin door was hanging wide

TERROR STRIKE

open.

"Maybe someone does live there," Jenny said.

"Maybe," Blade concurred, wondering if someone had found the cabin and moved in. What should he do if the place was occupied? The Founder had built the cabin, but no one from the Family had been there since the Big Blast. Could he rightfully claim it?

"How did you learn about this spot?" Jenny asked.

"Plato told me about it. The Founder used the cabin as a retreat," Blade explained, and pressed his right foot down on the accelerator. The Commando rested on the console between the bucket seats, and he placed his right hand on the weapon as a precaution.

"Maybe the cabin has been ramsacked," Jenny speculated.

"I hope not," Blade said. He drove along the western shore until the SEAL reached the field bordering the north end. Twenty yards off, at the edge of the forest, stood the cabin. He braked and shifted the transport into Park. "Stay here."

"I'll cover you," Jenny offered, leaning out her window, the Beretta in her hands.

"Watch out, Dad," Gabe said.

Blade nodded and climbed from the SEAL. He eased his door shut quietly, then advanced on the cabin. The structure appeared to be intact and sound, despite the passage of over a century. He stepped to within five yards of the doorway and halted. "Hello. Is anyone there?"

No one responded.

He trained the Commando on the door and cautiously moved closer, glancing at the windows on either side. The cabin seemed to be deserted, but there might be someone hiding inside. He edged to the right of the doorway and peered into the interior. His nostrils detected a distinct fishy odor, and his brow knit when he spied a pan resting on a stove in the northwest corner of the room. "Is anyone here?" he repeated. "I mean you no harm."

Again there wasn't any reply.

Strange.

Blade walked into the cabin, his eyes roving over the blue shag rug, the sofa, the bookshelf against the east wall, and the rocking chair, straight chair, and coffee table in the middle of the room. There was hardly any dust on the furniture or the rug, indicating someone had cleaned the place recently.

But who?

He moved to the kitchen area and noticed two dirty plates and silverware lying on a counter near the stove. A few pieces of dry fish remained in the pan on the stove. He reached out with his left hand and touched the pieces. They were cool, and separated into soft bits when he squeezed them, leading him to conclude that the meal had been cooked two or three days ago.

Where was the person who'd done the cooking?

"Hello," Blade declared, and angled to an open door on his right. He discovered a furnished bedroom, and he stared at the tidy bedspread in perplexity. The bed obviously hadn't been slept in, which only compounded the mystery. He went to each of the closets and cabinets, inspecting the contents, and was pleased to find the cabin fully stocked.

How weird.

From the evidence, he surmised someone had used the stove to prepare a single meal and then departed without pilfering any of the valuable items in the cabin. Such behavior was extraordinary. He turned from the closet in the southwest corner of the living room, bewildered that even the fishing tackle had been left alone, and his eyes strayed to the section of wall behind the open front door. There, leaning on the jamb, was a rifle.

Thoroughly confounded, Blade examined the weapon. He recognized the model as a Beeman/Krico Six Hundred. The Family Armory contained the same kind of weapon, and he'd fired it on a few occasions. He checked the three-shot detachable magazine and the barrel, and found the gun loaded and clean.

The enigma deepened.

No one in their right mind would go off and leave a perfectly good weapon, not in a day and age when a reliable rifle could mean the difference between life and death. Blade replaced the Beeman behind the door and stepped outside. He studied the grass and weeds in the vicinity of the entrance, hoping to find tracks. He located a few partial prints, but nothing unusual, nothing to explain the deserted cabin.

"Is it safe?" Jenny shouted.

Blade looked at the SEAL and nodded. He returned to his family, scrutinizing the small lake, impressed by the serenity of the scene. Two weeks at the retreat would give him the rest he sorely needed, but the puzzling state of the cabin bothered him. Was it really safe? None of the evidence conclusively proved foul play was involved, but the only reason he could conceive of for someone going off and leaving their rifle behind and the cabin door ajar was if the person had been slain. But if the occupant or occupants had been killed, why didn't the killer or killers plunder the cabin? Perhaps he was making the proverbial mountain out of a mole hill. There might be a perfectly innocent explanation. After all, as a Warrior he was inclined to evaluate every situation in terms of the potential for danger, and perhaps he attached too much significance to the gun, the open door, and the fish in the pan.

"What did you find in there?" Jenny inquired as Blade reached the driver's side.

"No one is home," Blade said. He took his seat in the SEAL and related the discoveries he'd made.

"It's sounds to me like someone left in a big hurry," Jenny conjectured when he concluded.

"But why?" Blade asked.

"Can we stay there until the people come back?" Gabe inquired.

Blade stared at the cabin, pondering their options. "I don't see why not. We've come this far, so we might as well enjoy ourselves."

"I agree," Jenny said. "If the occupants return, we'll explain the situation to them. I'm sure they'll understand."

"Then let's settle in," Blade proposed. He drove the SEAL to within a yard of the entrance and parked, aligning the transport so the driver's door was near the cabin doorway in case a quick exit became necessary. After switching off the ignition, he dropped to the ground, the Commando in his left hand.

Jenny and Gabe slid to the grass on the passenger side, and Jenny led their son inside to check out the interior.

The Warrior turned, surveying the surroundings, bothered by a vague sensation of unease, an inexplicable feeling that they were being watched. But there wasn't a soul in sight. He shrugged and went into the cabin.

"Oh, honey! This is wonderful!" Jenny exclaimed, delighted at the homey atmosphere. "I wish we had known about this retreat years ago."

"I'll begin unloading the things we need from the SEAL," Blade offered.

"From the looks of this place, we won't need much," Jenny said.

"Do you want me to bring in our spare clothes?"

"No. Just Gabe's pajamas. I can get whatever other clothes we need out of the SEAL anytime. But we'll need the brown bag containing our toilet articles. And don't forget the plastic jugs of water. Until we test the water here, we don't want to take any chances."

"Is that all?"

"Did you bring one of the flashlights?"

"Yes," Blade confirmed, knowing she was talking about one of the half-dozen flashlights the Family had received in trade with the Civilized Zone.

"We'll need the flashlight if we go outside at night," Jenny mentioned.

"Okay. Anything else?"

"Yeah. The food bag."

"But I told you about the canned goods in the cupboard."

"The way you two gorillas eat, I'll need all the food I can get," Jenny joked.

TERROR STRIKE 65

"All right. Now is *that* it?"

"It's all I can think of at the moment."

"Lucky me," Blade quipped. He slung the Commando over his left shoulder and returned to the SEAL.

The next several hours were spent at various tasks. Blade unloaded the SEAL and was conscripted to assist Jenny in washing every dish, glass, pot and pan, and piece of silverware in the cabin. Jenny replaced the sheets on the bed with a clean set she found in the bedroom closet. Because she wasn't quite satisfied with the cleanliness of the cabin, Jenny enlisted Gabe to give the place a dusting.

"We're only staying here for a couple of weeks, not a lifetime," Blade commented at one point.

"I refuse to sleep on a bed if I don't know who slept in it before me," Jenny said. "And I'm not about to use dishes and silverware any old scavenger might have used."

"I still think you're going overboard."

"Baloney. I keep our cabin at the Home this clean."

Blade glanced at his son, who was busy dusting the books. "I never realized you go to this much trouble."

"Of course not. You're a man."

"Meaning."

"Meaning men don't have the foggiest idea of how hard women have to work to keep a house neat and tidy. You think all we have to do is swish a dust cloth around and make a few passes with a broom and the place is spotless. But it doesn't work that way, especially if there are children in the family. A wife's work is never done."

"I try to help out," Blade said.

"You do," Jenny acknowledged, "when you're not off fighting dragons."

"I thought we agreed we weren't going to discuss my work once we got here?"

"Sorry," Jenny said.

"Hey, Dad?" Gabe interjected.

"What?"

"This is our vacation, isn't it?"

"Yeah," Blade replied.

"And didn't Mommy and you say our vacation is for having fun?"

"Yes," Blade responded.

"Then how come I'm not having fun yet?"

"Ask your mother."

Forty-five minutes later Jenny shooed them out of the cabin so she could prepare their supper in peace. She decided to open several of the cans in the cupboard to determine if the contents were edible, and began searching a drawer for a can opener.

Blade and Gabe strolled toward the lake. To the west the sun dipped closer and closer to the horizon.

"This place is neat," Gabe declared.

"You think so?"

"Sure do. Can we go fishing tomorrow?"

"First thing in the morning, unless your mom wants us to paint the cabin instead."

Gabe looked at his father in dismay. "Was that a joke?"

"Yep."

"Whew! You scared me," Gabe said.

Blade chuckled, stooped down to pick up a rock, and tossed it far out over the lake. He saw water spray upward as the rock splashed down.

"Dad, can I ask you something?" Gabe inquired.

"Anything."

"Why didn't you beat the crud out of the bad man today?"

"I wanted to."

"Why didn't you?"

Blade put his left hand on his son's shoulder. "Do you understand why I treated the man so roughly?"

"A little."

"I acted the way I did because the man wasn't treating your mom with the respect she deserves. He knew she's married to me, and yet he looked at her and talked to her as if she wasn't. I could tell he wanted her for himself."

"The bad man wanted to steal Mom?"

"In a way."

TERROR STRIKE

"When I get big, I'll beat the crud out of him for you," Gabe vowed.

"I doubt we'll ever run into him again," Blade said. "But remember what happened. One day you might find yourself in a similar situation. The relationship between a husband and a wife is very special, and you should do everything in your power to ensure others treat your wife with the courtesy she deserves. My dad told me there are certain rules a man should stick to if he wants to have a happy marriage."

"He did? Like what?"

"A man should never take his wife for granted. He should always treat his wife as his partner, not as a piece of property. Never keep a secret from your wife. And above all, never let anyone criticize her or abuse her," Blade recited from memory.

"Does Mom have rules too?" Gabe queried.

"I don't know. We'll ask her later. If she doesn't, she should," Blade said.

"Like what?"

"Let me see," Blade said, and scratched his chin. "A woman should never nag her husband. She should always be ready to sympathize with him when he stubs his toe. And she should always be in the mood when he is." He laughed and grinned.

"Was that another joke?"

"I wish it was."

They came to the edge of the water and halted.

"What kind of mood?" Gabe asked.

"Never mind. I'll explain when you're thirty," Blade said, and rested his hands on his Bowies.

"But I still don't get it. Why didn't you beat the crud out of the bad man?"

"Because I couldn't set myself up as his judge, jury, and executioner."

"Huh?"

"I made his punishment fit the crime. When someone oversteps their bounds and insults us or hurts us, we can't go overboard. We must always be fair in all our dealings with others, even when they're cow chips, as Uncle Hickok would say."

"I bet Uncle Hickok would've shot the bad man."

"Maybe. But Hickok would have given the man a chance to go for a gun. Uncle Hickok has his own set of rules he lives by."

Gabe gazed absently at the water near their feet, his young mind trying to comprehend the imponderable riddle of adult existence. "Does everyone have a set of rules they live by?"

"Nowadays most do. Before the war the situation was different."

"Why?"

"Before World War Three, most people lived by the rules set by the society they lived in. For instance, in America the people were regulated by hundreds of thousands of laws. The laws were the rules the people had to live by. If they broke the laws, they were punished by the legal authorities, by the government. The government used laws to control the people."

"The government controlled the people?"

"From the cradle until they passed on to the higher mansions."

"I don't think I would've liked living back then."

"Me neither. Nowadays everyone pretty much sets their own rules. But in California and the Civilized Zone the governments have a lot of laws, like America did, because California and the Civilized Zone have a lot of politicians. Politicians love to make laws."

"What's a politician?"

"They claim to be public servants, to serve the will of the people, but a lot of them serve themselves. They're always trying to get richer or become more powerful. In the worst cases, politicians are second-rate power-mongers. Always remember, Gabe, that laws are the chains power-mongers use to enslave people."

"Are all laws bad?"

"No. Just as all politicians aren't bad. There are a few sincere ones who want to do good."

"Why don't we have any at the Home?"

"Because the Founder warned the Family not to allow a professional political class to be developed. Being a power-monger is one of the few grounds for expulsion, for being kicked out of the Family," Blade said. "Our Founder never liked the fact that politicians in his time expected to be treated as if they were special. They always had special titles, and they allowed themselves special privileges. In the end, right before the war, the politicians had set themselves up as a special class above the ordinary citizens. Kurt Carpenter never wanted that to happen at the Home."

"I'm glad I live at the Home," Gabe remarked.

"That makes two of us."

They strolled to the east, covering a dozen yards, gazing over the lake.

"I bet there are big fish in here," Gabe declared.

"We'll find out tomorrow."

"Are there fish big enough to eat me?' Gabe asked.

"I doubt it."

"But what—" Gabe began, when a shout from the cabin cut him short.

"Gabe! Blade! Time for supper!" Jenny yelled.

"Good. My stomach is growling," Blade commented. He turned on his heel and strode toward their vacation hideaway. "Come on, son."

"Dad!" Gabe suddenly cried.

Blade spun. "What is it?"

"There!" Gabe declared, pointing at the lake, at a point 20 feet away. "Did you see it?"

"What?" Blade responded, scanning the surface and finding nothing unusual. He could see the bottom out to 15 yards or so.

"The biggest fish in the universe! It was bigger than me. Almost as big as you."

Blade smiled. "You're starting early."

"What?"

"Most fisherman don't start telling tall tales until they're a little older," Blade said.

"But I saw something," Gabe insisted. "It was big and dark and swimming under the water."

The Warrior scrutinized the lake. "Whatever it was, it's gone now. Let's go eat."

They walked off, with Gabe constantly glancing over his right shoulder.

"Do you believe me?" he asked.

"Of course. Now we know there are big fish in the lake. We'll catch one tomorrow morning and Mommy will cook it for lunch."

"If the thing doesn't eat us first."

CHAPTER SEVEN

Their evening supper consisted of venison sandwiches Jenny had packed for the trip, along with a can of green beans and, for dessert, a can of peaches, both of which she took from the cupboard. After their meal, Blade carried an empty lantern he found on the kitchen counter into the bedroom, where several cans of kerosene were stored in the closet. He filled the lantern, lit the wick, and walked to the living room to deposit the lantern on the coffee table.

"I'll do the dishes," Jenny volunteered.

Blade sat in the rocking chair and gazed out the left-hand window at the lake. Twilight had descended, enveloping the landscape in shadows. He saw several ducks alight on the water and paddle about. Behind him arose the clatter of dishes as Jenny cleaned their supper plates. "I like it here," he announced.

"So do I," Gabe stated. He moved around the rocking chair and stepped to the left window, blocking Blade's view.

Jenny started humming.

Feeling content and peaceful, Blade closed his eyes and

rocked slowly back and forth.

"Where'd he come from?" Gabe unexpectedly asked.

The Warrior's eyes snapped open. "Who?"

"That man."

"What man?" Blade demanded, rising.

"The man standing in the water."

Blade was to the open door in two long strides. He stood next to the left jamb and stared at the lake, but there wasn't anyone in sight. "Where? I don't see a man."

"He was there," Gabe asserted. "Standing near the shore."

Blade's eyes narrowed. He discerned a series of concentric ripples approximately ten feet from the north shore. "What happened to him?"

"He went under the water."

Jenny came over and joined them. "What's going on? Is there really somebody there?"

"I saw him," Gabe said.

The Warrior waited expectantly, his eyes ranging from one end of the lake to the other. Nothing moved. Even the ducks had disappeared.

"Perhaps you saw a shadow. The light can play tricks on you at this time of the day," Jenny postulated.

"I saw a man," Gabe maintained, his tone signifying his hurt at not being believed.

"Wait here," Blade directed them. He advanced to the edge of the water, unslinging the Commando as he crossed the field. The ripples had subsided and the surface was placid. He tried to peer into the depths, but the growing darkness had transformed the underwater domain into a murky realm shrouded in secrecy. What could Gabe have seen? he asked himself. The boy never lied. But if there had been someone in the water, whoever it was should have surfaced for air. Puzzled, he wheeled and took several steps, engrossed in contemplation.

"Blade! Look out!" Jenny abruptly shouted.

"Dad!" Gabe screeched.

Blade looked at his loved ones, who had come around the

TERROR STRIKE

front of the SEAL, and saw Jenny pointing to the west. He spun, leveling the Commando, hearing the patter of onrushing pads as he rotated.

There were three of them, bounding at the Warrior in a concerted charge, their tails held horizontally. Their coats were a grizzled gray. They stood over three feet high at the shoulder and weighed at least 120 pounds apiece. Flowing over the ground at 30 miles an hour, they growled as they closed on their prey.

Wolves!

A pack of gray wolves!

There was scarcely time for Blade to wonder why the wolves were attacking him. Wolves seldom went after humans unless they were starving or provoked, and the trio bearing down on him appeared to be healthy specimens. But not for long. They were 15 feet away when Blade pressed the trigger and the Commando thundered and recoiled in his arms.

The heavy slugs tore into the pack, perforating each animal repeatedly as the Warrior moved the barrel from right to left. The rounds thudded into the wolves and bowled them over. All three sprawled onto the ground, and only two attempted to scramble to their feet and renew their charge.

Blade wasn't about to let up. He aimed at the pair and fired another burst. One toppled, but the remaining wolf kept coming, and was now less than eight feet from the Warrior's legs.

"Blade!" Jenny screamed.

The Warrior held the Commando steady and kept the trigger depressed, his legs braced, his back to the water. Every shot hit home, smacking into the last wolf's head, dissolving the eyes and the forehead in a geyser of blood and gore.

With a final defiant snarl the wolf fell.

Blade let up on the trigger, his ears ringing from the din of the sustained burst. He edged to the nearest wolf and nudged the body with his left foot, then walked to the other two and checked them for life. All three were dead. Completely mystified by their unexpected attack, he gazed thoughtfully at the last animal. A stillness had descended upon the Northern woods.

Jenny and Gabe ran toward him.

Why? the Warrior asked himself. Why did the wolves try to slay him? If they weren't hungry, what was their motive? Had one of them been shot by a human before and as a consequence they despised all humans? Had they mistaken him for someone else?

A loud splash, accented by the deathly quiet, came from the lake.

Blade turned and beheld a commotion in the water less than ten feet from the shore, as if something large swam near the surface.

"Are you all right?" Jenny asked, hurrying to his side, holding Gabe by the left hand and the Beretta in her right.

"Fine," Blade said.

"Why'd they try to kill you, Dad?" Gabe questioned.

"I wish I knew."

Jenny glanced around nervously. "We should get Gabe back to the cabin. There's no telling what else might be in the trees."

The Warrior nodded. Animals and mutations for miles around must use the lake to quench their thirst, and since most predators were more active at night, he wanted his family safe and sound while the nocturnal beasts were abroad. "To the cabin," he said. "I'll bury these carcasses in the morning."

"Maybe the man in the lake will eat them," Gabe stated.

"Don't start that again," Jenny told him.

Together they returned to the cabin. Blade verified the SEAL was locked, then bolted the cabin door and inspected the metal latch on every window.

"You can leave a window cracked open," Jenny suggested. "We can use fresh air in here to dispel the fish smell."

"Not tonight," Blade replied, slinging the Commando over his left arm as he took a seat on the sofa.

"Why not? Wolves can't open windows."

"Tomorrow night, if we're still here, we'll crack a window.

TERROR STRIKE

Tonight I intend to play it safe."

Jenny's forehead creased. "Do you know something I don't?"

"No."

"Did you see something outside?"

"No."

She pursed her lips, looked at Gabe, and wisely dropped the subject. "I have a great idea. Why don't we play a game?"

"What kind of game?" Gabe responded.

"I'll show you in a second," Jenny said, and stepped into the bedroom.

"While you're in there, grab another lantern," Blade called out.

Gabe came over and sat down alongside his father. "Are we going to stay here?"

"I don't know yet," Blade said.

"What if there are more wolves?"

"Normally wolves leave human beings alone unless they're starving," Blade answered, and instantly regretted his lack of tact.

"Were those wolves starving?"

Blade looked at his son and debated whether to lie or tell the truth. Years ago he had resolved never to lie to his children, and he answered accordingly. "No."

Gabe considered the information for several seconds. "Dad, I don't know if I want to stay here very long."

"We'll see how everyone feels in the morning."

Jenny ambled from the bedroom, smiling broadly, the picture of cheerfulness. In her left hand was the lantern Blade had requested. She raised her right hand and opened her palm. "Look at what I found in the top drawer of the dresser! A deck of cards."

Blade glanced at the cards, then at his wife. Was she really as happy as she appeared, or was she putting on an act for Gabe's benefit?

"We can play cards for a few hours and turn in," Jenny proposed. She deposited the lantern on the kitchen counter and faced them. "What will it be? Gin rummy? Hearts? Poop on Your Neighbor?"

Gabe stood, brightening considerably, and grinned. "What's that game we play where we say, 'Go fish'?"

"You want to play that one?"

"Yeah."

Jenny looked at Blade. "Well, Mister Doom-and-Gloom? Are you going to sit there scowling all night, or will you lighten up and join us?"

"Deal me in," the Warrior said, his mouth curling upward. "But give me a minute." He walked to the counter and examined the second lantern, which turned out to be empty, then entered the bedroom to fill the circular tank with kerosene. After lighting the wick he grabbed the handle in his left hand and went out.

Gabe and Jenny were sitting on the floor next to the coffee table. She was shuffling the cards while he watched intently.

"Gabe, isn't there something we must do before we play cards?" Blade asked.

"Like what?" Gabe replied innocently.

"You know what," Blade said.

"What?" Jenny chimed in.

"What do you think?" Blade rejoined.

"I don't—" Jenny started to respond, and her gaze drifted to a point several inches below Blade's belt. "Oh. That's right. Gabe, you haven't gone since we arrived. You must need to go to the bathroom."

"I can wait," Gabe said.

"I can't," Blade stated, "so we might as well go together. Come on. Help me find a suitable tree."

"I don't want to go into the woods," Gabe declared.

"That was a joke."

"Oh."

Blade moved to the door and threw the bolt.

"Why don't you take the flashlight?" Jenny asked.

"I want to conserve the batteries," Blade said. He didn't bother to add that the flashlight was small and the beam of light it projected was thin. The lantern illuminated a greater area, although the illumination didn't extend as far as the flashlight beam, and he preferred to have a wider field of fire if necessary.

Father and son left the cabin and walked to the right, around the southwest corner.

Gabe stared at the inky wall of vegetation to the rear of the cabin and halted. "Let's go right here."

"We shouldn't go this close to the cabin."

"Why not?"

"It's not sanitary," Blade said, and walked to the west, paralleling the towering trees.

Gabe's wide eyes were riveted on the forest. He tried to glue himself to his father's right leg, gripping the fatigue pants with both hands.

"Are you scared?" Blade inquired tenderly, and stopped 30 feet from the log building.

"Nope," Gabe replied quickly, too quickly. He gazed up into the kindly face above him. "That's not true. Yeah, Dad, I'm scared. I'm sorry." His voice wavered as he spoke the last two words.

"What do you have to be sorry about?"

"For being scared. For not being brave like you," Gabe said softly.

"I've been scared plenty of times."

"You have?" Gabe responded in astonishment.

"More times than I care to count."

"But I didn't think you ever got scared. Ringo says his dad is never scared."

"And Ringo is right about his dad. Your Uncle Hickok is one of the few genuinely fearless people I know. Hickok will walk into danger with that devil-may-care grin of his plastered on his ugly puss because he takes everything in stride. Absolutely everything. In fact, I'd go so far as to say that Hickok is probably the bravest Warrior the Family has ever known."

The conversation had temporarily soothed Gabe's qualms.

"Wow!" he exclaimed. "Is Uncle Hickok braver than you are?"

"In one sense, yes."

"I don't understand," Gabe said.

Blade scanned their immediate vicinity, ensuring they were alone. "Let me give you an example. Let's pretend Hickok and I are going to fight a band of raiders."

"How many raiders?" Gabe asked.

"I don't know. The number isn't important."

"Yes, it is," Gabe insisted. "How many?"

"Oh, let's say there are forty raiders."

"Gosh! That's a lot."

"You bet. And it's Hickok and me against all of those raiders. Now let's pretend the raiders have us surrounded and there's nothing we can do but fight. Hickok would tear right into them without a second thought. He wouldn't worry about being shot or stabbed. He wouldn't give any thought to the odds. And it would never occur to him to be afraid. But I'd be different," Blade said, and paused. "I'd be calculating the odds and worrying about being outnumbered and outgunned. I'd be afraid of being injured or killed. Most of all, I'd be afraid that I'd never see your mom and you again. But even though I was afraid, I'd be right by Hickok's side. Despite my fear, I'd do what had to be done. That's the measure of a man's courage, Gabe. When a person admits their fears and confronts their fears head-on, that's true courage."

"Do Geronimo and Rikki and Yama get scared too?"

"Geronimo and Rikki, yes. I don't know about Yama any more. Ever since we came back from the run to Seattle, Yama has been acting like he's invincible."

"Then it's okay for me to be scared?" Gabe asked.

"Yes. Just try not and let your fear get the better of you. Conquer your fears and you conquer yourself."

Gabe nodded knowingly, as if his youthful mind comprehended every word his father uttered. "Can I tinkle now?"

"We'll both tinkle."

They watered the weeds and retraced their steps toward the cabin. Blade saw Jenny watching them through the west window. They were almost to the southwest corner when a tremendous tumult erupted in the lake, a noisy splashing intermixed with a panicked bleating.

"Get inside," Blade ordered, and moved with his son to the doorway where Jenny awaited them. "Stay put," he said, and jogged across the field to the water, the lantern swaying in his left hand and causing the light to dance eerily about him as he ran, the Commando in his right. He discerned the outline of shadowy forms struggling in the lake, perhaps 15 yards from the north shore. The bleating grew weaker and weaker with every passing moment. He tried to identify the source, and the first animals that came to mind were sheep and goats, but he knew the guess was ridiculous because there weren't any sheep or goats within miles of the retreat. The only other likely candidate he could think of was a deer. A very terrified deer.

Blade focused on the thrashing and held the lantern higher, but the radius of the light fell slightly short of the disturbance. He glimpsed a swirling of limbs and heard a final, pathetic bleat, and whatever was creating the commotion sank beneath the surface. He waited, hoping the deer, if such it was, would resurface, hoping to get a clue as to what was going on.

Nothing happened.

"Blade?" Jenny shouted.

The Warrior frowned, gave the lake a last searching glance, and hastened to his loved ones.

"What was it, Dad?" Gabe asked when his father was still 20 feet away.

"I think a deer tried to swim across the lake and didn't make it," Blade said.

"A doe or a buck?" Gabe queried.

"I couldn't really tell," Blade said.

"The poor deer," Jenny commented.

Blade perceived the relief on their features at the mundane explanation. He smiled and motioned at the cabin. "Didn't I hear someone say something about a game of cards?"

CHAPTER EIGHT

She moved with an obvious urgency in her stride, her loose-fitting orange dress a distinct contrast to the enveloping night. Her usually calm hazel eyes were troubled and her oval face set in lines of worry. The red hair topping her five-foot frame was stirred by the cool night breeze. She gazed absently at the stars and prayed the man she needed to see would still be up.

There was his cabin!

She stopped for a second, surprised to find him seated in a wooden chair a yard from his cabin door, his head tilted back so he could view the celestial spectacle. "Plato?"

The Family Leader shifted in his chair and looked around. "Who—?"

She advanced and announced herself. "It's me. Hazel. What are you doing out so late?"

Plato stood and regarded her quizzically. "My favorite pastime is to commune with the Spirit at night. I feel closer to our Divine Source when I'm viewing the immensity of creation."

TERROR STRIKE

"I understand. I feel the same way."

"And to what do I owe this honor, Hazel?" Plato inquired.

"The chief Family Empath is seldom abroad at this hour."

"I needed to talk to you," Hazel replied, her eyes straying to the cabin. "Is Nadine still up?"

"My charming wife retired a half hour ago. She's keeping the bed warm for me."

"Good. I wouldn't want to disturb her."

"I can get you a chair from inside," Plato offered.

"No. I'm fine."

"Suit yourself," Plato said, and clasped his wiry hands behind his back, waiting for her to broach the subject that had brought her to his doorstep at such an unusual time. They had known one another for five decades, and he realized that whatever prompted the visit must be crucial. As one of the six Family members gifted with psychic abilities, and the most sensitive of the group, Hazel had been of incalculable benefit over the years in periods of crisis.

"Blade and Jenny left on their trip this morning, didn't they?" Hazel questioned.

"Yes," Plato said, concern flaring within him. "Why?"

"Do you know where they went?"

"To a lake about ten miles northeast of the Home, and they don't intend to return for at least two weeks."

Hazel sighed and gestured at the chair. "I could use a seat after all. Do you mind?"

"Help yourself," Plato replied, stepping aside so she could sit down.

"Do you have any way of contacting Blade?" Hazel inquired.

"No."

"He didn't take along a radio?"

"No. He wanted his family to enjoy their trip without any interference. Jenny was looking forward to this vacation and he didn't want anything to spoil it for her."

Hazel stared at the ground.

"Why all these queries involving Blade? Is his family in

any jeopardy?"

"I don't know," Hazel said hesitantly.

"Uncertainty brought you here so late? Explain yourself, Hazel," Plato directed.

She nodded and looked at him. "Yesterday morning, twenty-four hours before Blade departed, Eva came to me and related a disturbing dream she had the night before. The dream baffled her because she dreamt about Blade, which she had never done.

"What was the nature of her dream?"

Hazel coughed lightly and averted her gaze. "Eva said the dream was short but intensely vivid. In it, she saw Blade swimming in a body of water, when suddenly he sank below the surface and kept sinking until he touched bottom. He kept trying to swim back up, but try as he might he couldn't." She paused. "He drowned."

"Why wasn't I informed about this dream?" Plato asked.

"One dream in and of itself is not especially significant. You're undoubtedly well aware of the random nature of most dreams. Quite frequently dreams will be precipitated by the food we ingest before we retire. Or our emotional state will influence the dreams we experience. As a group, we Empaths evaluate dreams in conjunction with other factors to determine the validity of the vision," Hazel related. "Of course, had I known Blade was planning to spend his trip at a lake, I would have attached more importance to Eva's dream."

"Blade wanted the destination kept secret so he could surprise Jenny," Plato mentioned.

"I see," Hazel said.

"The dream alone wouldn't have brought you here," Plato noted. "What else has occurred?"

"Several hours ago I retired. I had spent most of the day assisting the Weavers in making new quilts, and I was very tired. I fell asleep right away, and I experienced a distressing dream."

"Involving Blade?"

TERROR STRIKE

"Yes. I saw him driving the SEAL. He came to a clearing and parked, and Jenny, Gabe, and Blade got out to stretch their legs. Jenny strolled near some trees, and when the others had their backs turned, someone or something reached out of the trees and grabbed Jenny, covering her mouth so she couldn't scream. A bit later, while Blade was inspecting the underside of the transport, Gabe was snatched. Blade realized they were missing and went searching for them, and I saw a gun barrel poke out of the underbrush to his rear," Hazel detailed somberly.

"What happened next?" Plato prompted.

"There was a shot and Blade pitched forward, shot through the head. And then I heard a wicked laugh, an evil sort of cackling that became louder and louder until I woke up with a start," Hazel said, and stared at him. "Plato, the dream was exceptionally graphic. I awoke terrified by what I'd seen."

"And you believe Blade and his family are in definite danger?"

"I believe there is a strong possibility, yes. Which is why I came to see you. I haven't been this upset by a dream in years. Taken in conjunction with Eva's vision, there is serious cause for alarm," Hazel stated.

"Damn!" Plato said, venting a rare oath.

"What will you do?"

"My options are limited. Obviously I must send someone after them. But there are no roads into the area where Blade has taken his family. Whoever goes after them will have to travel overland and contend with the wild animals, the mutations, and all the rest."

"Which makes it a job for the Warriors. Send Hickok," Hazel suggested.

"Nathan is in charge of the Warriors in Blade's absence. He must stay here."

"Any of the Warriors would be happy to warn Blade," Hazel said.

"True. But I need someone who can cover the distance between the Home and the lake quickly. Someone who can run for hours without tiring."

"Yama can," Hazel mentioned.

"Yes, Yama is one of the few Warriors whose physique is almost as powerfully developed as Blade's. But Yama has been behaving oddly since that business in Seattle. I'm thinking of someone else, someone as strong as Yama and as dedicated as Hickok."

Hazel glanced to the south. "Oh. Him."

"You don't agree with my choice?"

"On the contrary, if anyone can reach Blade quickly, it would be him."

"I must speak to him immediately. Do you want me to walk you to your cabin?"

"No, but thanks for the offer," Hazel said. "Before you go I want to apologize. I should have consulted you after Eva's dream instead of waiting this long. I'm sorry."

"You conducted yourself properly," Plato assured her. "We'll discuss this further tomorrow, if you wish."

"Fine."

"Now if you'll excuse me," Plato said, and hurried to the south along the row of cabins. Because he had learned to trust Hazel's intuitive premonitions, anxiety seized his mind. He blamed himself for the situation. He was the one who had initially proposed the idea of using the founder's retreat to Blade, so the burden must rest on his shoulders. Any trip beyond the walled security of the Home entailed grave risks, as he well knew. But he'd believed that Blade could handle any problem, any threat. Perhaps he'd been lulled into complacency. Perhaps he'd allowed his confidence in Blade's prowess to subvert his better judgment.

Plato passed Blade's empty cabin and glanced at the darkened windows. If the giant Warrior or his family came to any harm, Plato would never forgive himself. He affectionately thought of Blade as the son he'd never had, and they enjoyed a strong bond of friendship. If Blade died, Plato would be torn to the depths of his soul.

TERROR STRIKE

He passed other cabins as he continued southward. The lights were out at Hickok's but on at Geronimo's, and he was tempted to stop and relay the news to Geronimo, but he refrained. Geronimo would undoubtedly want to inform Hickok, and the stubborn gunfighter would probably insist on sending out a rescue team immediately. Plato intended to talk to Hickok in the morning, after a night's rest girded him for the ordeal. Provided he could sleep.

Minutes later he spied his destination, and he paused when he saw the lanterns weren't on. If he knocked now, he might rouse the children. But if he wanted the Warrior to leave at daybreak, then he had to inform the man now. Plato walked to the cabin and rapped lightly on the door. After 30 seconds elapsed and no one answered, he knocked again, louder.

Still no one came.

Plato raised his right hand to knock even harder.

The cabin door abruptly swung inward and the barrel of a Bushmaster Auto Rifle poked out.

"It's only me!" Plato blurted out as the barrel came to within inches of his nose.

"Plato?" a deep voice said, and the Bushmaster lowered.

"Yes. I'm sorry for this intrusion," Plato stated, looking at the Warrior's face, striving to distinguish details in the dark. All he could discern was the Warrior's long, flowing hair and massive wide bulk.

"Is the Home under attack?"

"No, nothing like that," Plato replied. "I need you to go on an urgent mission at first light."

"Where?"

"Blade and Jenny have gone on a trip to a lake ten miles northeast of the Home, and I have reason to believe they may be in danger. You must travel to the lake and ascertain if they are safe."

"I'll be ready to leave at dawn. Has Hickok been informed?"

"No, not yet."

"I can't leave without notifying him."

"I know. I'll meet you at his cabin shortly before first light and clear your departure with him," Plato said.

"Fair enough. You sound very worried about Blade. How serious is it?"

Plato shrugged. "I don't honestly know," he admitted. "The Empaths have given me reason to believe his life and the lives of Jenny and Gabe are imperiled. I just hope you can reach them before it's too late."

CHAPTER NINE

Blade came awake with a start and blinked a few times, clearing his mind of any residual sluggishness, remembering where he was and what had happened. He glanced at the faint sunlight filtering in the windows and shifted in the rocking chair, relieving a cramp in his lower back. Dozing in a chair all night was not his idea of a soothing sleep. He yawned and looked at the Commando in his lap, then at the bedroom door. Last night, before Jenny and Gabe retired, he'd positioned the rocking chair near the kitchen counter. From his vantage point he could see the bed where his wife and son lay sleeping, and he had an unobstructed view of the windows and the entrance. As much as he would have preferred to sleep in the bed, safety was his paramount consideration.

Outside the birds were coming alive and filling the forest with their lively chirping.

The Warrior stood slowly and stretched. He rubbed the prickly growth on his chin as he strolled to the door. He reached for the knob, then caught himself. First things first. Turning to the window on the left, he crouched and peeked over the sill at the field and the lake. Both presented a picture of peacefulness. A buck and two does munched on grass in the field, while a flock of nine ducks swam on the lake.

Blade stood and exited the cabin. He breathed in the cool morning air and wondered if he had allowed his imagination to get the better of him the evening before. In the warming light of a new day the setting seemed utterly harmless. He checked the SEAL, confirming no one had tampered with the vehicle during the night. Then he proceeded to the north shore, cradling the Commando in the crook of his left elbow, and as he started across the field the three deer took off for the shelter of the woods, the buck snorting and bounding high and the does trailing after him.

At the edge of the water Blade halted and watched the ducks swimming from west to east approximately 50 yards from the shore. He saw a large fish leap out of the lake, midway between where he stood and the ducks, and drop into the water again with a minor splash.

No wonder the Founder had used this spot as a retreat!

Blade was about to head back to the cabin when he remembered the three gray wolves and turned, expecting to see the trio of bodies lying where they had fallen.

The wolves were gone.

The Warrior examined the ground carefully. He found puddles of blood where the three wolves had lain for hours, but there were no marks to indicate the direction the carcasses had been dragged. If they *had* been dragged. He made a tight sweep of the field near the lake, but his hunt for tracks proved fruitless. The wolves would have been tempting meals for any hungry animal or mutation, so the absence of the bodies was not in itself noteworthy. The lack of prints and drag marks, however, was bizarre. What, he asked himself, could have lifted the wolves and carted them off? Certainly nothing on four legs could have performed the feat. Even if a cougar or, as was extremely unlikely, a bear had lugged the bodies into the forest, there should have been evidence of some kind. Neither a cougar nor a bear would be capable of lifting the body of a full-grown wolf completely off the ground.

Wait a minute.

What was he doing?

Blade chuckled and shook his head, amused at his attempt to construct a menacing scenario out of the simple disappearance of dead wolves. He strolled in the direction of the cabin, admiring the natural splendor of the setting, and gazed to the east at the rising sun. Last night he'd been ready to leave; now he wasn't so sure. He decided to try his hand at fishing and make up his mind about departing after breakfast.

Jenny was waiting for him in the doorway, dressed in a white robe, her hair disheveled. She stifled a yawn as he came around the SEAL and looked at him anxiously. "Anything?"

"Nothing."

"Nothing?" she repeated quizzically.

"The wolves are gone, but anything could have taken them. I'm going to grab a pole and go fishing."

"Is it safe to stay then?"

"For the moment."

Jenny fussed with her hair. "Should we head back to the Home today?"

"I don't know. What do you think?" Blade asked.

"Why don't we stay half the day at least. I mean, except for the wolves and the strange noises we heard, which could have been a deer in the lake, there's no reason to leave. I don't want to cut our vacation short."

"Then we'll stay until noon, possibly longer," Blade said.

"Good. I'll get dressed and wait for you to catch some fish. Don't forget to clean them," Jenny said. She grinned and winked at him, then headed for the bedroom.

Blade slung the Commando over his left shoulder, took one of the fishing rods from the closet in the living room, and returned to the lake. Digging for worms proved to be easy, and during the next 30 minutes he caught five fish. Whistling to himself, he used the end of the fishing line to string the fish and carried them to the cabin.

"Gabe is still asleep," Jenny announced when he walked in the door.

"He was up late last night," Blade remarked.

"Those two hours of cards did the trick. He was laughing and having loads of fun by the time we hit the sack," Jenny said. She stared at the fish and scrunched up her nose. "Why aren't those fish clean?"

"I thought I'd clean them on the kitchen counter," Blade responded.

"You thought wrong. The last sight I want to see in the morning is fish guts."

"I bet Cynthia would clean them," Blade mentioned playfully.

"You're not married to Cynthia," Jenny stated.

"I know. Geronimo has all the luck."

Jenny stuck out her tongue and held up a long, thin knife. "Look at what I found."

"Is that to trim your toenails?"

"No, dummy. You know perfectly well what it's for. Now take those fish out of here."

Blade took the knife, kissed her on the forehead, and went outside, angling to the west. Twenty feet from the cabin he deposited the fish on the grass and knelt. Jenny's quirk about fish had always tickled him. She could skin a deer or pluck a grouse without a problem, but slicing into a fish and removing the stomach and the spine nauseated her. She'd tried on several occasions, and each time with the same results. He remembered a particular instance when she had bisected a trout and peeled the two halves apart, and there was a worm inside the fish, wiggling and squiggling. The shriek she'd voiced had nearly shattered his eardrums.

He laughed at the recollection and went about cleaning the fish, stacking the prepared sections in a pile. As he began inserting the knife into the last fish an ominous event transpired.

The birds in the forest abruptly ceased singing and the insects stopped buzzing.

TERROR STRIKE

Blade tensed and glanced at the woods, probing the undergrowth. Every seasoned woodsman knew to beware if the wildlife suddenly fell silent. Usually the silence betokened the presence of a meat-eater.

Even the trees were still, the air momentarily motionless.

Blade released the knife and gripped the strap to the Commando, and as he did the forest again became filled with the sound of the wild creatures. The various birds were especially noisy, singing their welcome to the new day. He waited for another interruption in the rhythm of the woodland, but all appeared well. After a bit he finished the fish and carried them to the cabin. "Here we go," he said when he stepped through the doorway.

"Look who's up," Jenny stated.

Gabe stood by his mother's side near the bedroom door, his eyelids drooping drowsily. "Hi, Dad."

"Hi, sleepyhead," Blade responded, moving to the kitchen and depositing the fish on the counter. "Here you go, honey."

"Thanks. How would you like fried potatoes and toast with your fish?"

"How would you like a nibble on your neck?" Blade answered jokingly.

Gabe glanced at his father. "Why would you want to nibble on Mommy's neck?"

"Now see what you've done," Jenny said.

"Go get dressed," Blade told his son.

"Why would you want to nibble on Mommy's neck?" Gabe repeated.

"That was another joke," Blade explained.

"I don't get it."

"All I meant was that I'm so hungry I could eat Mommy's neck if she doesn't fix breakfast fast," Blade said.

Jenny snorted and went to work on the meal.

"Why would you want to eat Mommy's neck?" Gabe inquired.

"I don't really want to," Blade admitted.

"You're worse than Hickok," Jenny muttered.

Gabe looked from one parent to the other, then shook his head and shuffled to the bedroom. "That was a dumb joke, Dad."

"Do me a favor," Jenny said softly.

"What?" Blade asked.

"When Gabe finally expresses curiosity about the birds and the bees, let me tell him about the facts of life."

"Why you?"

"Because men have a tendency to distort the truth."

"We do not."

"Oh, yeah? Hickok told Ringo that babies are delivered by storks."

"I'm not Hickok," Blade noted.

"No. You'll probably tell Gabe babies are delivered by mastodons."

"Now why would I do something that silly?"

Jenny shrugged as she arranged plates on the counter. "If I knew the answer to what makes men tick, I'd be the wisest woman on the planet. No woman can claim to understand men."

"Why not?"

"Two reasons. One, men and women are two distinct varieties of the same species. From birth and throughout all eternity we're completely different. We can think alike at times, and even appreciate each other on emotional, intellectual, and spiritual levels, but we can't totally comprehend everything because of our separate natures."

Blade waited for her to continue, and spoke up when she didn't. "You said there were two reasons but you only mentioned one. What's the other reason men and women can't fully understand each other?"

Jenny looked at him and smirked. "Men are weird."

"Women," Blade mumbled, and turned, walking idly toward the from door. He was five feet from the entrance when the left-hand window exploded inward, showering shards of glass in all directions, and something thudded into the bookcase. For a second he gaped at the shattered window, astounded, and then his years of training and experience came into play and he pivoted, his ears belatedly registering the crack of the shot, and darted to the kitchen.

Jenny was standing behind the counter, a frying pan in her left hand, her mouth hanging open.

Blade reached the counter and shoved her down. "Get on the floor!" he cried, and out of the corner of his right eye he detected movement. He spun, his heart seeming to pump harder at the sight of Gabe coming from the bedroom, confusion twisting his features, his pants on but his shirt bunched around his neck.

The boy blundered into the line of fire from the left-hand window, not a foot from the bookcase.

"No!" Blade bellowed, and hurled himself at his son, his arms outstretched.

A chip of the remaining glass flew from the window and the second shot boomed outside.

Blade felt a stinging sensation in his right shoulder. His arms looped about Gabe and he pulled his son to the floor, rolling as he hit, taking them to the right. He stopped in the middle of the floor and pressed Gabe flat on his stomach.

"What's going on?" Gabe asked, a tremor in his tone.

"Stay down," Blade instructed him. "Someone is shooting at us."

"Who?" Gabe asked.

"I don't know," Blade said, and glanced at the kitchen counter. "Jenny, are you okay?"

"No."

For a moment Blade thought she'd been hit, and a chill rippled down his spine. "You're not?"

"No, I'm ticked off. I dropped the fish on the floor."

The Warrior didn't know whether to chew her out or laugh, so he compromised and snickered. Then he focused on the left-hand window, wondering if there would be another shot.

"What should we do?" Jenny queried.

"We don't do anything until I assess the situation," Blade replied.

They stayed on the floor for several minutes, but the firing did not resume.

"Don't budge," Blade ordered his son. He crawled to the front door and swung it closed, half expecting the sniper to send a round into the cabin in response, but nothing happened. Using his elbows to pull himself along, he moved to the window and slowly, ever so cautiously rose to his knees.

"Be careful," Jenny advised.

Blade looked over his left shoulder. His wife was lying flat on the floor with her head protruding past the end of the counter. He blew her a kiss, then eased his left eye to the corner of the window. The front of the SEAL, part of the field, and the lake beyond were all visible. He guessed that the sniper was hidden in the tall weeds somewhere between the SEAL and the water. But where? He scrutinized the field.

"Anything?" Jenny whispered.

Blade drew away from the sill and gazed at her, shaking his head.

"Maybe whoever it is has gone," Jenny said without a shred of conviction.

As, if in answer to her speculation, a third sharp report sounded and a bullet punched through the top panel of the door, inches from the roof, sending wood chips flying.

Blade hugged the floor and fumed.

CHAPTER TEN

He covered five miles without incident.

In stature he reached three inches above six feet, but his massive, superbly muscled, broad-shouldered build lent him the illusion of being much taller. His alert brown eyes swept the terrain ahead. He breathed easily, his square jaw set firmly, jogging at a tireless dogtrot. Light brown hair hung to the small of his wide back, braided from the neck down. A camouflage outfit tailored to fit by the Family Weavers covered his solid form. And a pair of Bushmaster Auto Pistols adorned his waist, one in a specially crafted swivel holster on each hip. Slung over his right shoulder was his Bushmaster Auto Rifle.

Five miles or so to go, he told himself.

The day promised to be a hot one, and the warm sunlight combined with his exertion had caked him with sweat. He swiped at beads of perspiration on his brow and skirted a high pine tree.

A startled squirrel scampered out of his path and climbed up the pine, venting its annoyance with a vehement chittering.

He smiled and pressed on, thinking of Naomi, Benjamin,

and Ruth, of their sad expressions when they had seen him off at the drawbridge. "The Lord will watch over me," he had assured them, but his words of inspiration had not alleviated their distress.

Far overhead a hawk circled, seeking prey.

The Warrior came to a hill and headed for the top, his brown leather boots thumping on the ground. The sound reminded him of the angry blow Hickok had delivered to the side of his cabin during the heated argument with Plato. He'd dutifully stood to one side and listened, knowing it was not his place to interrupt. Plato had been quite insistent on the need for his departure, and equally insistent that only one Warrior should make the journey. Hickok had argued that several Warriors should go, that there would be safety in numbers. But the Family Leader had pointed out there was only one other Warrior who could cover ten miles cross-country at a steady pace, namely Yama, and Yama was on wall duty. Hickok had volunteered the services of the hybrid Warriors, the three mutations. Unfortunately, the hybrids were on a two-day break, and had ventured to Halma to assist the Clan in exterminating a wolverine that had raided a few outlying residences. Plato prevailed, and Hickok reluctantly agreed to send just one Warrior.

He considered Plato's confidence in his ability a distinct honor.

A bald clearing crowned the hill, marked by a few small boulders. A badger squatting below the rim saw him coming and immediately backed into a nearby burrow, hissing and squealing.

The Warrior ignored the animal and started to descend the hill. To take his mind off his family and the mission, he mentally began to recite his favorite passages from the Bible. Paslm Eighteen came to mind: "I will love thee, O Lord, my strength. The Lord is my rock, and my fortress, and my deliverer; my God, my strength, in whom I will trust; my buckler, and the horn of my salvation, and my high tower. I will call upon the Lord, who is worthy to be praised: so shall

I be saved from mine enemies." How true, he noted, and then abruptly stopped.

Something had growled.

He lowered his hands to his sides and scanned the brush and trees. A dark four-legged form moved through the undergrowth to his right, a large, bulky thing with a shuffling gait, then disappeared.

Another guttural growl sounded.

The Warrior refused to be delayed. He angled to the left, intending to bypass the creature in the woods. He kept his eyes on the spot where he had seen it last, and consequently he neglected to pay proper attention to the slope he was traversing. His right boot bumped into an object and became entangled. He fell forward, looking down to see the tip of his boot hooked in the supple branches of a knee-high bush, and landed on his hands and knees. His boot was wedged in the bush, but he wrenched his foot free and went to rise.

Just then a terrible roar rent the forest.

He rose, spinning as he straightened, his hands dropping to his Bushmaster Auto Pistols. He'd designed the swivel holsters personally, and the Family Gunsmiths had constructed the pair to fit his requirements. All he had to do was grasp the synthetic pistols' grips and swing the barrels upwards, and both breakaway holsters would part at the seam, allowing him to fire from the hip. He'd practiced and practiced until he could perform the technique swiftly and efficiently, and his practice now served him in good stead.

A raging mutation burst from the undergrowth, a deformed monstrosity of a black bear, its head misshapen, its shoulders forming a hunchbacked peak, its left limbs shorter than its right.

The Warrior stood firm, resolutely facing the charging beast. Both Bushmasters were attached to their swivel holsters by a stud affixed to a slotted metal plate so he could tilt the guns as high as needed. He angled the barrels and squeezed both triggers.

Lumbering and snarling, the bear advanced awkwardly, its

body rising and falling as its uneven limbs made contact with the earth. Because the bear's parents had been affected by the lingering radiation poisoning the ecological chain, the animal had been born with only one eye instead of two. The solitary orb was situated in the center of its forehead, giving the beast a Cyclopean appearance. Its nostrils were half the length they should be and flattened at the end, almost piggish in aspect. Many of its upper teeth were inches too long and jutted over its lower lip, vampirelike. When the first rounds bored into its head and chest, the bear recoiled, roared again, and came on even faster.

He never expected the beast to reach him. There were 30 shots in the magazine of each Bushmaster, and there wasn't an animal living that could absorb 60 rounds and live. Or so he believed.

But the bear, rushing headlong down the slope, took all 60 and never slowed. Crimson-speckled holes dotted its head and torso, yet its spark of vitality was undiminished.

The Warrior realized the bear would get to him when it was only three yards away, and he released the Bushmasters and braced his legs. The mutation slammed into him going at full speed, and the impact lifted him from his feet and sent him tumbling down the hill. He flipped end over end, completely disoriented, until he crashed into the trunk of a tree with a bone-jarring concussion. Dazed, his ribs in agony, he pushed himself to his knees and twisted in time to see the bear still on its feet and coming at him with its jaws wide. He tried to dodge to the right, but the bear plowed into him once more and he was flung back against the tree. This time his head made violent contact and swirling stars engulfed his mind as something heavy pounced on his back.

The Warrior passed out.

CHAPTER ELEVEN

"It's been hours. The sniper must have gone," Jenny commented hopefully.

"Can we try and get in the SEAL now, Dad?" Gabe asked.

Blade glanced at them and pondered their next move. True, six hours had elapsed and it was almost noon. And the last time the sniper had fired had been three hours ago, when Blade had tried to reach the transport. He'd opened the front door and poked his head out, and a bullet had missed him by less than an inch, smacking into the jamb and spewing tiny wood fragments onto his hair. He'd slid back inside and slammed the door shut.

For three hours there had been quiet. Blade had moved Gabe behind the kitchen counter, and his wife and son lay side by side watching him expectantly. "I'll take a look," he told them, and crawled toward the door. His plan to park the SEAL close to the entrance so he could reach the vehicle quickly in an emergency had backfired. Yesterday he had locked the doors to ensure no one could enter the transport during the night, and now those locked doors were thrwarting his efforts to escape. A yard of space separated the SEAL from the cabin. The sniper, after firing those initial rounds, had changed position to cover the front door clearly, shifting somewhere to the east, still hidden in the thick weeds. As Blade had learned when he stuck his head out, the rifleman now commanded a perfect shot at the space between the vehicle and the doorway. In the five seconds Blade would need to step to the SEAL, insert the key, unlock the door, and climb inside, the sniper would be able to squeeze off several shots. Even if Blade tried to sneak out the west window and come around the rear of the SEAL, the sniper would still spot him and cut loose. He was willing to take the risk, but Jenny protested and he'd respected her wishes for the time being.

Blade came to the door and stopped, the Commando in his hands in front of him. Several conclusions were obvious. There was only one sniper. Only one gun had fired each time, with the recognizable blast of a high-powered rifle. Since the person doing the shooting had persisted until midmorning, and was probably still out there, the sniper wasn't about to be discouraged easily. And since the assassin could have waited and picked off one of them when they stepped outside instead of firing randomly through the window, the sniper must be toying with them, playing a bizarre sort of demented game. Cat-and-mouse, and they were the mice.

Blade squatted and clutched the doorknob. If he'd been by himself he would have gone out one of the windows hours ago and tried to circle around and find their assailant, but he knew Jenny and Gabe wanted him to stay. Jenny put on a brave front, but she wasn't accustomed to combat and the strain showed in her eyes and her drawn features. Gabe, surprisingly, had recovered from his first fears and was bearing the strain better than his mother.

He turned the knob, shoved, and flattened.

No shot greeted his action.

Blade raised his head and inched to the doorway. He

extended the Commando barrel out and instantly withdrew it.

Still nothing happened.

Had the sniper tired of the game and departed?

Blade squatted with his back to the right jamb and contemplated. He wondered if the man Gabe had seen at the lake was the same one shooting at them. Perhaps the sniper lived at the cabin and was striving to drive them off. But if that were the case, the man wouldn't prevent them from getting into the SEAL and leaving. Was the rifleman a long raider, a rogue, or simply a solitary psychopath who got his kicks by gunning down others?

"Are you going out?" Jenny inquired. She was kneeling next to the counter, holding the Beretta. Gabe peeked over her left shoulder.

"I may," Blade replied. "Whatever happens, the two of you must stay inside. Agreed?"

"What if you're hurt?" Jenny inquired.

"I'll take care of myself. You two must stay in the cabin, no matter what. I can't cover myself and protect you at the same time."

"We'll stay here," Jenny said.

Blade nodded, bent over, and stepped to the coffee table. He seized one of the legs in his left hand and moved to the south wall, standing between the door and the left-hand window.

"Be careful, Dad," Gabe said.

The Warrior smiled at his family, then whipped his left arm in an arc and spun, flinging the coffee table out the shattered window. As his fingers released the coffee table he darted out the doorway and ducked to the right. Hopefully, the sniper had focused on the table and would need a second to react. Blade raced to the southwest corner and swung around, his back to the west wall.

The sniper hadn't fired!

Blade grinned and sighed in relief. Either he'd taken the

bastard by surprise or the sniper was gone! He headed to the north, pausing to glance in the west window and wave at Jenny and Gabe. Jenny spotted him first, nudged their son, and they both waved and smiled. He ran to the forest and took cover behind a tree.

So far, so good.

If his estimation of the sniper's last position was correct, he should be able to find where the sniper had been concealed in the weeds. With that as his goal, he moved through the woods to the east, staying five yards from the edge of the field. Once past the cabin he could see the section where the rifleman must have been hidden, and he crouched and studied every bush, every clump and patch, for any evidence of the sniper.

Nothing.

Encouraged, Blade crept to the tree nearest the field and hunkered down. A robin winged from a pine tree off to his left toward the lake. He eased onto his elbows and knees and snaked into the field, moving at a turtle's pace, endeavoring to minimize the rustling he caused, pressing on the weeds as lightly as possible.

Somewhere a cricket chirped.

Blade traveled 15 yards, constantly glancing at the cabin, until he reached a point where the space between the SEAL and the front door was visible. He examined the ground minutely, them moved slightly farther east. In two yards he found what he was looking for, an area several yards long and 18 inches wide where the weeds had been flattened by a heavy body lying on them for hours. A flash of reflected sunlight arrested his attention, and he discovered a spent cartridge. He picked up the metallic brass casing and turned it over to check the caliber, which was .30-06. That didn't help him much. There were too many rifles capable of firing .30-06 rounds for him to be able to identify the weapon from the casing. He dropped the cartridge on the ground and swiveled toward the cabin.

What should he do next?

He was tempted to return to his family, pack them in the SEAL, and get out of there. But he had to ensure the sniper was definitely gone before exposing them outside. He elected to conduct a sweep of the field and the lake.

The minutes dragged by as Blade conducted his search, crossing and recrossing the field in a zigzag pattern until he came to the border of the water. He rose to a crouch and surveyed the land rimming the lake. The sniper's disappearance puzzled him. He couldn't bring himself to accept that the sniper had really departed. Since the man had vacated the field, he must be in the forest.

Blade made a beeline for the trees, dashing through the weeds while stooped over at the waist, and he attained the woods without being fired upon. More time passed as he prowled the undergrowth, and after 20 minutes he hiked back to the cabin, finally convinced the phantom rifleman had slipped away. Now he intended to rev up the SEAL and make tracks for the Home. Enough was enough. First Gabe had seen things in the lake, then the wolves had tried to kill him, and now this! Vacations weren't all they were cracked up to be. He might as well be on a run with the Warriors for all the rest he was getting.

The sun had peaked at its zenith an hour ago.

Blade moved along the west wall and rounded the corner. As he walked past the right-hand window he glanced inside and saw Jenny sitting in the rocking chair and Gabe in the straight chair. Both were facing the doorway. Why, when he had specifically instructed them to remain behind the counter, had they disregarded him? He stepped into the cabin and they looked at him in fear, and before he could open his mouth a rifle barrel jammed him roughly in the back of the head.

"Don't move, you big son of a bitch!"

The Warrior tensed at the sound of the familiar voice, the same nasal twang he'd heard the day before at the scavengers' camp.

"Let your submachine gun fall to the floor," the man behind him ordered.

Blade complied, lowering the Carbine slowly.

"Now put your hands on top of your head."

Again, frowning, his eyes on his frightened wife and son, he obeyed.

"You aren't so tough, scumbag," the man said, and came around the Warrior with his rifle leveled.

Blade glared at the weasel, his eyes slits of rage.

"You remember me, don't you? Roy. The guy you beat the crap out of yesterday for no good reason."

The Warrior refused to respond.

"Yeah, you remember me, sucker," Roy declared spitefully. "You thought you were so high and mighty, pounding on me because I looked crosswise at your squeeze. Well, you ain't so high and mighty now, are you, turkey?"

Blade glanced at Jenny and Gabe.

"Sorry, honey," Jenny said. "He caught us off guard."

"You bet your ass I did!" Roy stated, gloating, staring contemptuously at the Warrior. "Do you want to know how I did it?"

"I imagine you'll tell me," Blade responded.

"Damn straight I will," Roy said. He relished having the upper hand and being able to enact his vengeance, and he planned to savor his revenge to the final, sweet drop. "I was hiding in the trees when you went into the field, and while you were out there playing with yourself, I snuck to the west side of this dump. Then when you went into the trees again, I crawled to the front door and pretended I was you." He lowered his voice and spoke in a raspy whisper. "Jenny! It's me! I've been hurt. Help me."

Jenny bowed her head and closed her eyes.

"The bimbo and the kid fell for my trick," Roy said, and cackled. "They ran to the door and I shoved my gun in her belly and told them to listen or else. Pretty clever, huh?"

"It's me you want, not them," Blade mentioned. "Why

TERROR STRIKE

don't you let them go?" He spied Jenny's Beretta and Blackhawk on the sofa.

Roy snorted. "Do you expect me to let a fox like your woman walk on out of here? You're nuts. I aim to have a lot of fun with her after I'm done with you."

"You bad man!" Gabe shouted, tears of frustration welling in his innocent eyes.

"Shut your face, you little snot, or I'll waste you right here and now!" Roy snapped.

Blade gritted his teeth and measured the distance to the scavenger, gauging whether to make a desperate lunge. The weasel stood six feet away, two far to reach in one bound. If Blade tried, he would be shot. But he couldn't stand by helplessly while his family was abused. "You followed us all this way?" he asked, hoping to divert Roy's interest from Gabe.

"Following you was as easy as pie," Roy bragged. "That buggy of yours left a trail even an idiot couldn't lose."

"Then how did you manage?" Jenny baited him.

Roy sneered and took a stride toward her. "Open your mouth again, fuzz, and I'll put a bullet in your hubby. Right in the bellybutton. Do you know what a gut shot does to a man? He'll be in misery for hours, maybe days. He'll beg to be put out of his agony." He paused. "On second thought, smart-mouth me again. I want this prick to suffer before he dies."

"You realize this is a mistake," Blade interjected.

"Yeah. And you made it!" Roy responded maliciously.

"No, you did. Friends of ours are due to arrive here soon, within the hour. You'll be outnumbered."

"I don't believe there are any friends coming," Roy said. "You told Jared that you're on a special trip and you don't want anything interfering with it. No, your family is all alone here."

Blade scowled and absently flexed his arms. The man was a weasel, but a *smart* weasel. Blade couldn't afford to underestimate the scavenger again.

"We have the cabin all to ourselves," Roy noted. "Ain't it cozy?" He laughed wickedly.

"What about an exchange?" Blade asked.

"A what?"

"An exchange. A ransom. You already know the Family has a fully stocked armory. Why don't you trade me for all the weapons you want? They'd fetch a high price on the black market in any town in the Outlands."

Roy's forehead creased as he mulled the proposal.

"Just think. You could be rich. You'd be able to afford all the drink and women you desire. All you have to do is release my wife and son and let them drive to the Home. Someone will be sent with the ransom," Blade said, and looked at Jenny. He intuitively knew what she was thinking. She couldn't drive the SEAL. But the weasel wasn't aware of the fact. And he'd say or do anything to get his wife and son out of the cabin. If he could trick Roy into permitting them to enter the SEAL, they could lock the doors and would be protected by the transport's impregnable body.

"You must *really* think I'm a jerk if you expect me to fall for such a dumbass idea!" Roy declared.

"We'd keep our part of the bargain," Blade stated.

"The hell you would! Your Family would send a bunch of guys to off me. No dice, stupid. We're all staying right here. We'll even spend the night together," Roy said, and chuckled.

Blade envisioned the vile acts Roy had in mind, and his fury mounted. He couldn't tolerate the thought of Roy pawing Jenny. Sooner or later the weasel would get around to tying him up. He had to make his move before then.

"I have to go to the bathroom," Gabe unexpectedly announced.

"Tough, brat. Suffer," Roy responded.

"I'll pee my pants if I don't go," Gabe protested.

"Who the hell cares?"

"You're mean!" Gabe cried, and started to slide off the chair.

"Don't move!" Roy bellowed. He took a step in the boy's direction.

Blade saw his opportunity and leaped, his arms outstretched to swat the rifle aside. As if in slow motion he observed Roy pivot, and he watched the Ruger as the barrel swept up and pointed straight at him. His hands were nowhere near the rifle when the booming retort thundered in his ears and he felt the slug tear into his body.

CHAPTER TWELVE

He came awake slowly, painfully, his head throbbing, his consciousness seemingly floating in a stygian void. The exquisite agony almost overwhelmed him, and he struggled to rouse himself through sheer force of will.

Gradually his memory returned. He recalled the mutation, the monstrous bear. He remembered the fight and emptying both Auto Pistols into the creature. And he recollected colliding with the tree. Twice.

Now he felt the hard ground under his left cheek, and there was a great weight pressing down upon his back. He went to open his eyes, but couldn't.

For a second panic threatened to blossom, but he suppressed the fear and centered his concentration. Why wouldn't his eyes open? he asked himself. It felt like they were glued shut. He tried again, but the best he could do was crack the left eyelid a fraction, just enough to detect a glimmer of sunlight and realize the sun hadn't set. It was still daylight.

The Warrior tried to move his right arm, to wipe at his eyes, but the arm wouldn't budge. The enormous weight on top of him was pinning both arms. He attempted to slide his body to the side, but the weight prevented him, pinning him in place.

This wouldn't do.

He took a deep breath and thought, "I am yours, O Lord, to guide as you will. Grant your mortal son this request. Grant me the strength of my namesake."

The Warrior pressed both palms on the rough ground and pushed, his muscles straining. His shoulders and upper arms quivered. His nostrils flared as he breathed noisily. He succeeded in raising his head and chest an inch, but the burden on his back conspired with gravity and his pounding head to foil his intent. Dizziness washed over him and he sagged, a small rock gouging into his cheek.

He rested a moment, until the pounding subsided marginally, and experimented. His effort had not been in vain. Although his left arm was still pinned, he could move his right, and he brought his hand to his face and gingerly ran his fingertips over his features.

His forehead had been split open when his head smashed into the tree. He could feel the jagged wound, situated in the middle, running from his hairline almost to his nose, three inches in length and half an inch wide. The gash must have bled like a bear—he grinned at the thought—and accounted for the substance coating his eyelids. Most of the blood had dried, sticking his eyes shut. Most, but not all. He found a pool of blood ringing his head, more blood than he would have thought possible from such a wound, and he surmised the bear's blood must have seeped down and been added to his own.

He began peeling the dried blood from his eyelids, a tormenting process in itself. Every fleck he stripped off made him wince. His eyelids smarted terribly. In a minute he had his left eye fully open, and shortly thereafter, after using his nails to scrape off the blood adhered to his eyelash, he restored his right eye.

The Warrior took stock.

He was lying within six inches of the tree trunk, his body

aligned due north. The sun was well up in the sky, and he realized he'd been unconscious for hours. Turning his head to the left, he saw the front of the bear lying on top of his left shoulder. The mutation had fallen across him diagonally, which explained why the greatest weight was on his back and legs.

No wonder he couldn't rise.

Every second he was delayed increased the danger to Blade, Jenny, and young Gabe. Plato had told him about the Empaths' dreams and stressed the urgency of reaching Blade quickly. Despite the severe wound, no matter how much blood he'd lost, he had to continue. He had to replenish his depleted strength and energy.

There was only one way.

He placed his chin on the ground and closed his eyes, allowing himself to relax, and mentally probed deep within his mind for the spirit spark at the core of his being, the fragment of Deity he believed indwelt all men and women. Ever since childhood he'd been profoundly religious. At the Naming ceremony on his sixteenth birthday, the ceremony instituted by the Founder at which all Family members were encouraged to select their own names from any of the books in the library as a means of ensuring they appreciated their historical antecedents, he'd picked the name of one of the mightiest warriors in the Bible: Samson. Even earlier, at the age of seven, he'd publicly dedicated himself to the Lord by becoming a Nazarite.

The order of the voluntary Nazarites extended back into antiquity. Those who took the Nazarite vow pledged themselves to live according to the will of the Lord, every minute of every day. As part of the vow, as a physical symbol of his kinship to the Creator, Samson had promised to never permit a razor or scissors to cut his hair. He'd also taken an oath never to drink an intoxicating beverage. The original Samson, Samuel, and John the Baptist were just three of the renowned Nazarites mentioned in the Bible.

Like his namesake, Samson credited his virile vitality and

steely sinews to the fact he'd never broken his vow. Like the Samson of old, he knew all he had to do was call on the Lord and he would be granted the power to accomplish any task. So he called on the Lord now.

Samson placed both palms on the grass and surged upward, his arms exerting every iota of strength he possessed. His face turned red and his veins bulged. Ever so slowly he managed to rise himself an inch from the ground, then two, and three. Again vertigo engulfed him and he sank down.

He lay there, gathering his energy. If he wasn't weakened by the wound, he would have been able to shrug off the bear effortlessly. But now he had to focus on the indwelling Spirit as never before if he hoped to save his life and convey Plato's warning to Blade.

Samson tried one more time, ignoring the anguish, the torment racking his head, and threw his shoulders and back into the effort. The technique was the same as doing a push-up, he told himself. The only difference being that he was doing the push-up with a full-grown bear on his back.

"Hear my prayer, O Lord. Give me the strength of ten!"

He got his chest six inches off the earth. Every muscle on his body bulged and rippled. The dizzinesss recurred, but he shook his head, clearing his thoughts, striving to be at one with the limitless source of power within him.

"Your will be done, on Earth as it is in Heaven."

Samson grunted, pushing harder, getting his body a foot above the ground, but only from the knees up.

More!

He needed more!

"Hear me, O Lord! Fill me with the might of twenty!"

A current of immense force shot through his torso, recharging his flagging muscles, reviving his resolve. He tilted his head back, his mouth opening in a grimace, and surged upward, the sweat dripping from his brow.

"My cup runneth over!"

For a second his fate hung in the balance. He wobbled, the bear resting on his shoulders and back and threatening to dump him on his face.

Not again!

Samson trembled with the intensity of his monumental exertion. His fingertips were sinking into the dirt, and his knees felt ready to crack. "I am the Lord's!" he cried, and straightened, locking his legs and shoving.

The mutation tumbled to the earth.

The Warrior stood proudly erect, swaying slightly, elated by his victory. Tears of gratitude dampened his eyes, and he gazed at the azure sky, silently expressing his thankfulness. He wanted to spend an hour in proper worship, and he would once the mission was completed.

The mission!

Samson moved down the slope, unsteadily at first, his stride lengthening with every step. The loss of so much blood would slow him down for the next few miles. If another mutation should attack, he might well reach Blade too late, if he wasn't too late already. He estimated he wouldn't reach the lake until after dark.

What was he doing?

How could he be so careless?

He stopped abruptly and replaced the spent magazine in his Auto Pistols with fresh ones from the ammo pouch attached to the rear of his camouflage belt. Then he inspected the Bushmaster Auto Rifle and discovered blood caking one side of the weapon. A proper cleaning was in order, but it would have to wait.

Blade might be in trouble at that very minute.

Samson prayed his friend could hold out until he arrived, and resumed his trek to the northeast.

CHAPTER THIRTEEN

Blade heard the words dimly.

"—least let me bandage him!"

"He doesn't need a bandage, bitch. Just fix my grub before I blow the kid's brains all over this cabin."

"My daddy needs a Healer!"

"In a few hours your old man won't need diddly, brat. Now clam up or else!"

Blade breathed shallowly, endeavoring to recall what had happened. Why had he blacked out? Suddenly he remembered; there had been the shot and the shock of being hit, the torturous, searing pain as the bullet ripped through his midriff, and he had involuntarily doubled over, clutching his abdomen. Jenny had screamed, and he had looked up to see the stock of the scavanger's rifle sweeping at his head. He'd lost count of how many times Roy struck him. He didn't even recall slumping to the floor.

"Get me a glass of water," Roy directed.

Blade heard dishes rattling and he resisted the urge to open his eyes. He didn't want the bastard to know he was awake yet.

"Quit giving me the evil eye, brat, or I'll tie you up and throw you in the bedroom," Roy snapped. "No. I can't do that. Your mom and me are going to have some fun in there later."

"I hope my dad beats you to a pulp!" Gabe declared.

"Your dad's beating days are over, kid."

"If my daddy dies, the other Warriors will find you. Uncle Hickok will track you down and shoot you full of holes!" Gabe said.

"It's a big world, kid. Your dad's friends won't know where to begin to look."

"Uncle Hickok will never give up!"

"Shut up."

"Uncle Hickok will shoot you in the head!"

Blade heard the sound of movement followed by a sharp slap. He opened his eyes to behold Roy standing over Gabe, who sat on the straight chair with his right hand pressed to his cheek. Pride welled within him at the sight of his son sitting erect, glaring at the scavenger, unafraid.

"Leave him alone!" Jenny yelled, coming around the kitchen counter with a steak knife in her right hand.

Roy pointed the Ruger at her. "Back in the kitchen, whore!"

Blade was lying on his right side, facing the chairs, curled up in a fetal posture. The scavenger's back was to him, and neither Jenny or Gabe knew he had revived. He placed his right hand on the floor and tried to rise. To his surprise he felt little pain. Using both hands he rose to a crouch. He could feel a damp, sticky sensation on his stomach, but he refused to look down until after he accomplished what he had to do.

Jenny had stopped a yard from the counter, her face livid.

"Back in the damn kitchen!" Roy barked.

Blade clenched his fists and slid silently closer to the degenerate. A spasm lanced his abdomen and he gritted his teeth and suppressed an impulse to cry out.

"You know," Roy said as Jenny walked to the counter, "this isn't as much fun as I figured it would be. I thought I'd

TERROR STRIKE 115

toy with you turkeys for a day or so. Get my jollies. See the look on your husband's face when I stick it to you. Make all of you *suffer*!'' Roy hissed, and paused. ''But it's not working out the way I planned. The big son of a bitch might never open his eyes. I think I'll snuff the brat right now, then take you into the bedroom for a few hours, bitch.''

''I'd rather die first,'' Jenny said.

''Hey, one way or the other doesn't make any difference to me,'' Roy responded.

''You're sick.''

''Why? Because I take what I want? Because I kill to stay alive? It's dog-eat-dog nowadays, lady. Survival of the fittest.''

''You're disgusting because you enjoy inflicting pain on others. You terrorize and brutalize others to get your kicks. A real man would earn the respect and love of a woman, not take her against her will. But you're not a real man. You're not one of the fittest. You're nothing but a slimy pervert, and one day someone will squash you like the slug you are.''

''What a crock.''

''Mark my words,'' Jenny said solemnly.

''Nobody will ever take me down,'' Roy bragged.

''Wrong,'' stated the low voice behind him.

Roy whirled, bringing the rifle around, shuddering as he perceived the major blunder he'd made.

The Warrior uncoiled from his crouch with the speed of a striking cobra. The knuckles of his right fist caught the scavenger on the chin and propelled Roy into the air. Roy's teeth crunched together and blood spurted from his mouth.

''Blade!'' Jenny shouted.

The Warrior closed in as Roy toppled onto the rug. The scavenger landed on his back and attempted to scramble to his feet. Blade swung his left fist, driving the knuckles into Roy's nose, flattening the nostrils and sending Roy flying into the bookshelves. The rifle sailed to the right.

''Get him!'' Gabe cried.

Roy's elbows were hooked on the third shelf, supporting him, and he uttered a gurgling noise, his head bobbing, and turned.

Blade slammed his right fist into Roy's chest, and everyone in the room heard the loud crack. He followed through with a left. The scavenger buckled and fell to his knees.

"No more!" Roy blubbered. "Please!"

"For Gabe," Blade said, and delivered a right to the scavenger's left temple.

Roy toppled onto his side, the blood pouring over his lower lip, blubbering incoherently. He frantically heaved to his hands and knees.

"For Jenny," Blade stated. His left fist came down on Roy's back with the force of a pile driver.

The weasel was flattened by the blow. He screeched and crawled toward the bedroom. "Don't hurt me!"

Blade sneered and took a long stride, reaching down and locking the fingers of his left hand in Roy's oily hair. His grip slipped once, and then he tightened his hold and hauled the scavenger to a standing position. "This next one is for me."

"No!" Roy whined.

"Yes," Blade said coldly. He drew back his right fist, thinking of the abuse his loved ones had suffered, channeling his rage into the next punch, releasing the full extent of his fury. His fist smashed into the scavenger's mouth at the same instant he released Roy's hair, and the weasel flew backwards and thudded onto his back next to the bedroom doorway, limp and unconscious.

"Yah!" Gabe yelled.

Blade stared at his foe for a moment, then tottered, abruptly feeling weak. He hugged his abdomen and started to bend over.

"Honey!" Jenny exclaimed in alarm and dashed to his side. She looped her arms around his middle and helped ease him to the floor, where he could sit with his back propped against the east wall. "How bad is it?"

"Bad," Blade said.

"Don't move," Jenny instructed him. She ran to the kitchenette and began filling a bowl with water out of a jug they'd brought from the Home.

TERROR STRIKE

"Darn. I was hoping to do some calisthenics," Blade quipped feebly.

Gabe scooted to his father and knelt in front of him. "Dad, is there anything I can do?"

"Make sure that scumbag is out for the count," Blade said.

Nodding, Gabe stood and walked toward the scavenger.

"Here we go," Jenny stated, returning with the bowl of water and a clean washrag. "I'll remove your vest." She deposited the bowl and slowly unzipped Blade's black leather vest, frowning when she saw the blood rimming the top of his pants. Gently, exercising the utmost care, she unbuckled his belt and undid the button above the zipper, then eased the zipper down. Blood had soaked the fabric of his pants.

Filled by weariness, Blade leaned his head against the wall. He saw Gabe step behind the counter, then glanced down. "Have you found the entry hole?"

Jenny nodded and licked her lips. She pointed at the finger-sized hole three inches to the left of his navel. "It's stopped bleeding."

"That's good news," Blade said.

"Where's the exit hole?" Jenny asked, reaching gingerly around his back and probing with her fingers.

"I don't think there is one," Blade replied, and grunted.

"The bullet is still inside you?"

"I think so."

Jenny ran her fingers all over his lower back and finally withdrew her hands and placed them on his knees. "You're right. There's no exit hole."

"Damn," Blade said softly.

They both heard a loud, dull dong, as if a fractured bell had been struck with a hammer, and they looked at the scavenger.

Gabe stood over the weasel's head, the largest frying pan he could find in his slim hands. He raised the pan over his head a second time and brought the metal bottom down on the scavenger's forehead with all the strength he could muster.

"That should be enough," Blade said. "He's out for the

count."

"Maybe he's faking. I should hit him five or six times just to be sure."

"That's enough," Blade reiterated.

Gabe's disappointment showed.

"Tell you what, though," Blade added. "Why don't you stand guard over him. If he comes around or moves, let him have it."

"How many times?"

"Ten or twenty."

"I hope he moves," Gabe said.

Jenny leaned down and inspected her husband's belt, pants, and vest. "The Spirit smiled on you."

"Oh?"

"The bullet was deflected by your belt buckle into your belt, then passed through the belt and into you. It might not be very deep. If the buckle and the belt hadn't slowed it down, the bullet would have passed clean through and probably shattered your spine."

"You'll have to dig the slug out."

Jenny glanced into his eyes. "Me? I'm not a Healer."

"Gabe certainly can't perform the operation," Blade noted.

"But what if I do something wrong? What if I cut a vein or an artery or accidentally hit one of your organs?" Jenny asked, intimidated by the prospect of doing surgery.

"There's no one else who can do the job," Blade stressed. "The Home is too far away for me to risk the ride. Besides, if we wait, infection could set in."

Jenny swallowed hard. "If I make a mistake I could kill you."

"You must try, unless you like the idea of being a widow."

"Don't joke that way. It's not funny."

"I wasn't joking."

She stared at the entry hole, nervously rubbing her hands together. "What will I use for instruments?"

"We shouldn't need much. Since I've stopped bleeding and the entry hole isn't very large, we won't worry about stitches.

TERROR STRIKE

We'll need something to use as a probe and an instrument to cauterize the wound. Both have to be long and thin."

"I'll find what we need."

"The first step is to heat a pot of water to sterilize the instruments."

Jenny rose without another word and walked to the stove.

Waves of agony rippled over the Warrior and he gasped lightly so as not to cause any anxiety in his wife and son. Had the shot hit an organ? he wondered. If so, he needed to get to the Healers as swiftly as possible. He planned to take off for the Home after Jenny finished tending the wound, and he gazed at the front windows expecting to observe the bright sunlight of early afternoon. Instead there were shadows on the panes. "What time is it?"

"After six," Jenny answered, busy filling the pot.

"In the evening?" Blade asked in disbelief.

"Yep. You were out about five hours, more or less."

Five hours! Blade's shoulders slumped dejectedly. He wasn't about to try and drive to the Home in the dark, not in his condition, and Jenny undoubtedly wouldn't finish operating on him until nightfall. He swiveled his head to watch her. "What happened while I was out?"

"Not much."

"Did he lay a hand on you?" Blade queried harshly.

"He pawed me a few times, but he was more interested in gloating and baiting us. He deliberately tried to upset Gabe, to make him cry, but it didn't work," Jenny said. "I'm very proud of our son, and you should be too. He behaved like a man."

Still standing alertly over the scavenger, Gabe kicked Roy in the head. "He said bad words to Mom and kept touching her."

Jenny saw her husband's cheeks flush scarlet and changed the subject. "I fixed him a meal about half an hour after you were shot, and he was having me prepare another meal shortly before you woke up."

"He'll never eat again," Blade vowed.

"Stop talking and rest," Jenny advised.

Too fatigued to argue, Blade closed his eyes and wished they were all safe and sound back at the Home. With Roy out of commission they'd be safe at the cabin. Relatively safe, anyway. And in his current state nothing less than the walled security of the Home would alleviate his apprehension over not being able to protect Jenny and Gabe.

He glanced at the weasel, thankful the man was an idiot. An efficient adversary would have finished him off, murdered the others, and stolen the SEAL. Fortunately, Roy had been more interested in tormenting them than in attending to business.

"Say! I have an idea!" Gabe declared.

"What is it?" Jenny inquired while searching through a drawer for a suitable makeshift probe.

"I can go for help."

"You wouldn't be able to reach the Home on foot."

"Not to the Home. To those people we met. The nice people who were with the bad man."

"The scavengers?" Jenny said, staring at her son.

"Sure. They're not far. I can find them," Gabe said.

"They're a mile away, which might as well be on the moon for all the good they can do us," Jenny stated.

"I can do it!" Gabe asserted confidently.

"No," Jenny told him.

"But—" Gabe began, bubbling over with enthusiasm.

"No, son," Blade interjected. "It's almost dark, and you wouldn't be able to get to their camp before nightfall. There are more mutations and other predators abroad after the sun sets. You'd never make it."

"I'd try for you, Dad," Gabe said frankly.

The Warrior smiled, his throat constricted by an odd lump, his eyes dampening. "Thanks," he said huskily. "I appreciate the thought. But I want you to stay here with us."

"Okay," Gabe responded reluctantly.

Blade stared at the windows and reflected on his blessings. Despite the inconvenience of holding down two jobs, despite the periodic absences for days and weeks at a stretch, despite the stress his dangerous occupations caused, he had a wife and son who loved him with all their hearts, who would jeopardize their own lives to save his, who valued him more highly than life itself.

What more could any man ask for?

Jenny came over holding two objects in her left hand. "We don't have much of a selection to choose from. I've found forks, spoons, knives, scoops, basting brushes, and a few tools." She unfolded her hand to reveal an eight-inch Phillips screwdriver and a narrow butter knife. "They're both dull."

"They'll have to do," Blade said. "Use the screwdriver as the probe and we'll cauterize with the knife."

"*We'll* cauterize? What's this 'we' stuff? You'll lie there looking handsome and I'll be doing all the work." She wheeled and walked to the stove.

Blade grinned and rested his chin on his chest. His eyelids suddenly seemed to weigh a ton. Strange. He'd been shot several times during the course of his career as a Warrior and never reacted like this. Why did he feel so tired? He thought of the approaching night and wondered if the door had been bolted. When he tried to advise Jenny, however, all he could do was mumble. And seconds later he slumped onto his left side, oblivious to the world.

CHAPTER FOURTEEN

"We need more wood," Jared said.

"Don't we have enough already?" Tammy asked, gazing at the waist-high pile in front of them.

"The wind is picking up, which means our campfire will burn faster. If we run out of wood before dawn, someone will have to collect more. Do you want to walk around in the woods at night?"

"No," Tammy admitted, and faced the others. "You heard the man. We need more wood."

Jared looked at the sun hovering above the western horizon and made his way into the forest to the south, collecting suitble broken limbs as he went along. If only they'd been able to prevail upon Blade to take them to the Home instead of waiting for two weeks! A lot could happen in two weeks. There would undoubtedly be mutations to deal with, and who knew what else. He should have remonstrated with the giant, insisted tht they leave after Harold's burial. Tammy had acquiesced for fear of antagonizing Blade and ruining their golden opportunity to finally locate the famed compound, and he'd gone along

TERROR STRIKE 123

with her against his better judgment. Now he regretted his lack of resolve. The prospect of spending another night in the woods was distinctly unappealing.

A five-foot length of branch to his right drew his attention.

Jared stepped to the branch and bent down to retrieve it, when out of the corner of his right eye he saw a figure dart from one tree to another less than 30 feet away. He straightened, his pulse quickening, his mouth suddenly dry.

He let the wood he'd gathered clatter to the grass at his feet, and unslung his Marlin. The glimpse had been too fleeting to determine exactly who or what he'd seen, but of one fact he was certain: It wasn't one of his people. He backpedaled, angling in the direction of the camp, the hair at the nape of his neck prickling.

A feminine voice addressed him from the left. "What's this action, lover? We're collecting wood and you're practicing walking backwards?"

Jared glanced around and saw Tammy grinning at him. "We have company," he said.

She dropped her limbs and drew her Charter Arms Bulldog. "Friendly or hostile?"

"I don't know yet."

Tammy joined him and they hurried to the campfire, their eyes on the forest the whole time. Jim and Alice were depositing loads of wood and were about to venture out for more.

"Hold it," Jared said.

Jim took one look at Jared and unslung his Winchester. "What's up?"

"Keep your eyes peeled," Jared directed, and cupped his right hand to his mouth. "Everybody in! Forget the wood! Everybody back to camp!"

They waited expectantly for their companions to appear. Lloyd and his wife Betty emerged from the woods to the north, both carrying branches.

"What's going on?" Lloyd queried.

"Somebody's out there," Jared informed him.

The wood was forgotten as all six clutched their weapons and stared into the trees.

"I don't like standing next to the fire," Jim mentioned. "We make great targets."

"We'll wait for Tom, then take cover," Jared said.

"How many did you see?" Tammy asked him.

"One. Acting like he didn't want me to know he was there. Whoever it is might have been watching us for hours."

"Other scavengers, you think?" Lloyd questioned.

"I doubt it," Jared replied. "This area is too far off the beaten path for most scavengers. Hell, we wouldn't be here if we weren't looking for the Home. If it is scavengers, though, I doubt they'll give us any trouble unless they outnumber us."

"I've heard stories," Betty said. "Tales about hermits and backwoods types who prey on travelers."

"Why do you always look at the bright side?" Lloyd cracked.

"Where's Tom? He should have been back by now," Tammy noted.

"There he is!" Alice exclaimed, nodding to the west.

They saw their friend coming toward them, and they instantly perceived something was wrong. Tom walked in a slow, shuffling gait, his hands at his sides, swaying every few strides. His rifle and revolver were both gone.

"Tom?" Jared said, and took a step toward him.

Their companion came out of the shadows and lurched the final dozen feet. He collapsed onto his knees and arched his back, his mouth forming an O.

"Tom!" Jared reached his friend in two steps and went to loop his left arm about Tom's back, but his hand bumped into an obstruction, an object protruding from between Tom's shoulder blades. "Oh, no!" Jared declared.

Tom pitched onto his face. Everyone saw the slender shaft jutting from his back and the spreading crimson stain on his green shirt.

"An arrow!" Betty stated, aghast.

"And there's more where that came from!" bellowed a deep

TERROR STRIKE

voice from the undergrowth to the west. "Drop your guns!"

"Let's get the hell out of here!" Jim said, swinging around to the east.

They all heard the swish and thump, and they all saw the arrow penetrate Jim's forehead and bore out of the rear of his cranium. He stumbled backward for several feet and fell.

"Anyone who tries to run will be shot!" warned the voice.

"Jim!" Alice wailed, recovering from the shock of witnessing her husband's death. "Jim!" She spun to the east and fired two wild shots, working the bolt of her Mossberg rifle furiously.

Again a shaft streaked out of the woods, and again they heard the swishing noise, almost a buzzing, and saw the arrow catch her squarely in the chest, knocking her from her feet. Alice landed on her posterior and gaped at the six inches of shaft sticking from between her breasts. She glanced up at the others, said "Damn!" and died.

"We'll kill you all if we have to!" the voice threatened. "Drop your guns!"

Jared's mind was racing. There were only four of them left now, and there was still no telling how many enemies lurked in the brush. If all four made a break simultaneously, at least two would die. He didn't mind the idea of dying himself, but he couldn't abide the thought of harm coming to Tammy.

The lay of the land wasn't in their favor either. To the south the trees were sparse and the undergrowth thin, affording few hiding places. To the west, north, and east there were more trees, but there were also bowmen, one to the west, another to the east. Escaping to the north was their only option.

"I won't say it again! Drop your guns or die!" the man concealed to the west demanded.

Jared became aware of the others staring at him, awaiting his decision. He looked at Tammy sadly, frowned, and placed his rifle on the ground.

"We should fight!" Lloyd whispered.

"And wind up like Jim and Alice?" Jared responded, and let his revolver fall to the grass.

"You're being smart!" the voice told them. "All of you had better lay your guns down!"

Tammy, Lloyd, and Betty followed Jared's example.

"Now raise your hands over your head!" the man in the woods instructed them.

Jared extended his arms overhead and gazed at the forest, dreading that he'd committed a fatal mistake. He had no guarantee whoever was out there wouldn't slay them on the spot.

Two figures materialized in the brush, approaching warily, converging on the camp from both sides, one from the east, the other from the west. Both held bows. Each had an arrow ready to fly. The man to the west was taller and leaner. They sported scraggly dark hair down to their shoulders, and they wore crude clothing made from animal hides. The tall one had Tom's rifle over his left shoulder and Tom's revolver tucked under his homemade leather belt. A quiver full of arrows hung on the back of each.

"We've got us quite a haul," the tall one said, and laughed wickedly. He halted six feet from the quartet and scrutinized them closely. "Guns *and* women. Not bad."

"Who are you?" Jared asked, then added petulantly, "We aren't doing you any harm."

The tall one snorted. "Do you hear this fool, Silas? He says he wasn't doing us any harm."

Silas stopped eight feet from the campfire and shook his head. "How do some folks manage with such a pitiful shortage of brains, Harvey?"

"Beats me," Harvey replied, smirking at Jared.

"Please! Let us go!" Betty spoke up.

"You must be kidding, lady," Harvey retorted. "The slavers will pay us in gold for the redhead and you."

Jared's mouth curved downward and overwhelming regret flooded his soul. Lloyd had been right. They should never have given in without a fight.

"And all these weapons will keep us in food for months," Silas mentioned.

"Where are you from?" Tammy inquired, intending to distract the pair with conversation, her eyes on the Bulldog lying next to her right foot.

"Here and there," Harvey answered.

"Where are the slavers based?"

"On the moon," Harvey said sarcastically.

"Are there just the two of you?"

"Did you ever hear about what curiosity did to the cat?" Harvey responded.

Tammy realized the pair weren't about to divulge any information, and she thought about how she could grab the Bulldog without receiving an arrow through the chest for her effort. Sooner or later, one of them would lower his bow and reduce the odds against her by half. She knew if she didn't resist now, while she had the chance and her gun was within reach, she might spend the rest of her days in the clutches of a pervert.

"What about us?" Jared asked.

"What about you, asshole?" Harvey replied.

"What do you plan to do with us?"

"Not a thing. There's no market for men. The slavers are only interested in women."

"You're going to kill us!" Lloyd declared.

"Bingo," Harvey said, and released his shaft.

The arrow sped straight into Lloyd's torso, spearing into his heart, spinning him around and dropping him to the ground within a yard of the fire.

"Lloyd!" Betty screamed, and moved to his side. She knelt and placed her hands on his shoulders. "Lloyd!"

Tammy glanced at her Bulldog, girding herself to make the lunge.

"Don't even think it, bitch!" Silas warned, aiming his shaft at her.

Harvey pulled another arrow from his quiver and grinned at Jared. "Guess whose turn is next," he said, and notched the arrow on the bowstring.

Jared saw the tall man draw the string back and snicker.

He heard Betty weeping, and as he riveted his gaze on the razor-tipped hunting shaft he wondered if her plaintive crying would be the last sound he'd ever hear.

CHAPTER FIFTEEN

"Are you okay, Mom?"

"I'm tired, Gabe. Very, very tired."

"Will Daddy live?"

"If the Spirit is willing."

"When will Dad wake up?"

"I don't know," Jenny answered wearily. She walked to the sofa and sat down, sighing with relief, and stared lovingly at her husband. Blade was on his back on the floor near the bookshelves, his midriff tightly bandaged with strips torn from a clean sheet, covered from his toes to his chin with a brown blanket. His broad chest rose and fell gently.

Gabe stood next to the rocking chair, watching his father sleep, obviously worried. "Should we put him in bed?"

"How? He's too heavy for us to budge. No, he'll stay right where he is. Besides, we shouldn't wake him, son. He needs all the rest he can get. Thank the Spirit he passed out earlier and was unconscious during the operation. I know I would have caused him a lot of pain if he'd been awake."

"What should we do about the bad man?" Gabe inquired,

pointing at the scavenger.

Jenny looked at the battered, blood-caked, unconscious form and pursed her lips. She'd bound him securely, hands and feet, prior to ministering to Blade. Except for an occasional moan, Roy had not displayed any sign of life. Hatred billowed within her, an emotion she rarely experienced, and she wished the man was dead. He'd caused her family so much suffering! She ran her right hand through her hair, recalling the teachings of the Elders that love and compassion were two of the greatest mortal attributes and should be cultivated by all, and she felt a twinge of guilt over her hatred.

"What should we do?" Gabe repeated.

"I'll drag him outside in a minute," Jenny said.

"Will you put him in the SEAL?"

"No. I'll leave him on the ground alongside the transport."

"But what if an animal finds him, a wolf or a mutation?"

"Tough."

Gabe smiled and nodded. "You sound like Dad."

"Thanks for the compliment." Jenny opened her left hand and studied the bullet she'd pried out of her husband, trembling inadvertently as she mentally relived inserting the screwdriver into the entry hole. Five minutes of careful pushing and pressing had failed to locate the slug, so she'd resorted to using her fingers. Blade's skin had been extremely hot to her touch, a symptom of his high fever. She would never forget the soft texture of his flesh as her right index finger slid in and probed about.

"Can I see it?" Gabe asked, moving over and taking a seat on her left.

"Sure," she said, and watched him pick the slug up and examine it. "Thanks for helping me with the operation."

"Any time."

"Never again, as far as I'm concerned," Jenny said. She kissed him on the cheek, marveling at how composed he'd been while observing her pry the bullet out and later, when she'd cauterized the wound. He'd borne the grisly sights stoically and hadn't cried once.

"I think I'll sleep on the floor next to Dad," Gabe remarked.

She was about to tell him he couldn't, but she changed her mind. Since she intended to do the same, how could she justifiably refuse him permission? "We both will."

"When can we leave for the Home?"

Jenny gazed at the windows, noting the descent of twilight. "I don't know, honey. We're stuck here until your father is fit enough to drive. You know I can't."

"You could try," Gabe suggested.

"I've watched your father enough times that I probably could do a fair job, but I'm afraid of crashing us into a tree or a boulder. And what would happen if we were stranded in the middle of nowhere?"

"Aren't we stranded now?"

The question gave Jenny pause. She glanced at Blade, thinking of the consequences if he developed an infection. Gabe's idea tempted her. The Healers would have Blade on his feet in no time. But common sense prevailed. "It's not the same. At least here we can keep him warm and we have plenty of food and water. We're safe in the cabin."

"I'd feel safer in the SEAL."

Jenny stood and crossed to the scavenger, gazing at his crushed nose, split lip, black eyes, and puffy face without a trace of sympathy. She grasped him by the ankles and backed toward the front door.

"Can I help?" Gabe inquired.

"Get the door."

He scooted to the door, turned the knob, and pulled it wide open.

"Thanks," Jenny said. Her shoulders straining, she dragged the scavenger out and aligned him alongside the SEAL, next to the front tire on the driver's side. She stepped inside, bolted the door, and went to Blade to feel his forehead. His temperature seemed stable.

"Are you hungry, Mom?" Gabe queried.

"Are you?"

"Yeah."

"Then I'll rustle us up some food."

Jenny set to work preparing a can of chunky stew for their supper, trying to alleviate her anxiety by keeping busy. She repeatedly glanced at Blade, and memories of their marriage arose unbidden in her mind. She remembered how happy she'd felt when she gave birth to Gabriel, and the joy in Blade's eyes when he held his son in his arms for the very first time. She also thought about the time the Home had been attacked by the vicious Trolls from Fox, Minnesota, and of her capture and subsequent rescue by Blade. He was a devoted father and loyal husband. What woman could ask for more?

Gabe moved the rocking chair close to his dad and sat down, rocking and watching Blade's face. "Mom, can I ask you a question?"

"Certainly."

"Where do we go when we die?"

The unexpected query made her do a double take. She leaned on the counter and regarded Gabe intently. "Why do you ask?"

"I want to know."

Jenny looked at Blade, worried that Gabe might be expecting his father to die. "Well, you've asked a very important question. All down through the ages men and women have wondered about the same thing. There have been a lot of different ideas about where we go after we die, and yet despite the differences they all pretty much agree on one point."

"How do you mean?" Gabe inquired earnestly.

"I'm not an expert, you understand. You should talk to Plato or Joshua. They know more about religion and philosophy than I do. But I do know the Bible teaches that we pass on to Heaven. The Koran says we'll live in Paradise. Most religions agree that we survive this life and ascend to a higher spiritual level."

"What do *you* think?"

"I believe the Elders when they tell us that we'll awaken in the mansion worlds on high. I believe there's a part of us, our soul, that becomes one with the Spirit and lives forever."

"Does Daddy believe like you do?"

"More or less, yes."

"So if Daddy dies and goes to the mansions, we'll see him again someday?"

"Yes. When we die, we'll join him on the next level."

"Does everybody who dies go there?"

"The Elders say a person has to have faith to survive."

"What's faith?"

Jenny made a smacking sound with her lips. "You sure ask the tough ones. Faith is belief in the Spirit."

"Do I have faith?"

"You believe in the Spirit, don't you?"

"I think so."

"You've listened to Joshua and the Elders talk about God. Do you believe there is a God?"

"Yep. But I don't know what God is."

"You're still young. Give yourself another fifteen or twenty years. A person can't be expected to wrestle with profound spiritual questions until they're mature enough to understand the answers."

"Huh?"

"You believe there's a supreme Spirit. That's enough for now. You have nothing to worry about because you'll pass on to the next level."

"Good," Gabe said, and gazed at his father. "Dad believes in the Spirit, right?"

"Of course he does."

"And does he believe in the things the Elders say about loving everyone?"

Jenny saw what was coming and smiled. "Yes."

"Then how come he kills bad people?"

"Because they *are* bad people. Your father believes that the spiritual have the right and the duty to protect themselves from those who aren't spiritual, from those who are deliberately evil, from those who enjoy being wicked. That's why the Warriors were formed, to protect the Family and the Home from those who would destroy both. Believe it or not, there are some who want to wipe out our Family. There have always been those, Gabe, who live a life of spite and hatred, devoted to destruction," Jenny paused. "Do you understand any of this?"

"I think so. I hope I can become a Warrior when I'm big and protect the Home like Daddy does."

"Maybe you will," Jenny responded. She checked the stew on the stove, pleased with herself for being able to answer his questions so well. "The stew is hot. Are you ready to eat?"

"You bet."

Jenny found two bowls and ladled the piping hot stew into them. Minutes later she and Gabe were seated on the floor next to Blade, spooning the broth and vegetables into their mouths.

"Ummmm. This is tasty," Gabe said.

"Thank the folks who made this a hundred years ago."

Gabe studied the stew for several seconds and his forehead creased. "How come canned stuff lasts so long?"

"Some does, some doesn't. We know canned goods are more likely to be edible if they've been stored in a cool, dry place. The age doesn't seem to matter, only where the canned goods are stockpiled."

They continued eating in silence.

Jenny swallowed the last of her helping and looked at the front windows. Darkness enshrouded the land, and she could barely distinguish the huge bulk of the SEAL a yard from the cabin. "I'd better light the lanterns," she proposed, and walked to the counter to set down her bowl.

Something thumped against the west wall.

"Did you hear that?" Gabe asked.

"Probably just the wind," Jenny said. She lit the lantern Blade had placed on the counter first, then the lantern on the coffee table. As she blew out the match and straightened, the thump on the west wall was repeated.

"Do you want me to go see what's doing that?" Gabe asked hopefully.

"No. We're staying right here."

"Maybe it's an animal."
"So?"
"I can chase it away."
"It'll go away on its own. We're not going outside unless you have to go to the bathroom."
"Not right now, Mom."
"Then how about a game of cards?" Jenny recommended.
"Sounds great."

Jenny picked up the deck from the coffee table and glanced at her Beretta, which was leaning against the kitchen counter. She doubted the wind accounted for the pounding on the cabin. A curious bear might give a building a few whacks, and curious bears were better left to wander off and amuse themselves elsewhere.

"Did you hear that?" Gabe suddenly asked, standing.
"What?" Jenny replied, cocking her head to listen.
"That," Gabe said.

And she heard it too, a low, pathetic cry from out front, the words barely audible.

"Help me!"

"It's the bad man!" Gabe exclaimed.
"I know," Jenny said, having recognized the voice.
"What do we do?"
"We play cards," Jenny stated, and sat down alongside the coffee table.

Gabe hesitated, his eyes on the left-hand window, waiting to hear the cry once more. But a minute elapsed and nothing happened. "Okay." He took a seat across the table from her. "You deal."

"You trust a cardsharp like me?" Jenny joked.
Gabe chuckled. "You wouldn't cheat."
"Why not?"
"You're my mom."

Jenny laughed and went to cut the deck.

"Help me!"

They both looked at the front door. The plea had been louder and laced with sorrow.

"Shouldn't we help him?" Gabe questioned.

"No. He probably just wants water, and he can die of thirst for all I care," Jenny snapped.

"Help me! Please! Something is out here!"

Jenny twisted, staring out the window behind her. "What did he say?" she asked, although she knew very well what the scavenger had said.

"Something is out there," Gabe said nervously.

"He's lying to make us go out. There's nothing out there," Jenny stated.

"Are you sure?"

"Do you trust that man after what he did to us?"

"No, I guess not."

"Then let's forget about him and play cards," Jenny advised, cutting the deck as loudly as she could.

"Please! There's something out here! It's looking at me!"

"Be quiet!" Jenny shouted angrily. "You're not fooling us! Shut up and leave us alone!"

"Please! I'm not making this up!"

"Quiet!" Jenny yelled.

"Maybe we should take a peak," Gabe suggested.

"No."

"Dad would take a peak."

"Your dad would break his face," Jenny declared. She began dealing the cards out. "Now concentrate on the game and forget about the S.O.B."

"What's an S.O.B.?" Gabe inquired innocently.

Jenny frowned, annoyed at herself, then mustered an easygoing grin. "S.O.B. stands for Selfish Obnoxious Boob."

"Really? I never heard that one before."

"Just don't use it in public."

"Why not?"

"Because some people don't like to be called selfish," Jenny answered. "Now let's play cards."

The scavenger abruptly shrieked in terror. *"Dear God! It's coming toward me! Please get out here! Help! Help!"*

Jenny slammed the cards on the table and stood. The last

cry had bordered on the hysterical. She retrieved her rifle and hastened to the door, loosening the .44 Magnum in its holster.

"Can I come?" Gabe asked, rising.

"Stay here," Jenny said, her hand on the doorknob. She wanted to ignore the man, to believe his cries were a ruse to lure them outside, but the panic in his voice persuaded her he was telling the truth. And no matter how much she despised him, she couldn't sit idly by while an animal ate him alive.

"Be careful," Gabe said.

"I will," she promised, and let go of the knob to throw the bolt. "Lock this behind me."

Gabe watched her step out and close the door quickly. He stared at the windows, hoping to see her appear and wave, indicating that everything was fine, but she didn't. He moved toward the door to obey her instructions, then paused. What if she got into trouble out there? What if she needed to return in a hurry? The smart thing to do was leave the door unlocked.

A muffled exclamation sounded from near the entrance.

"Mom?" Gabe called.

Dark forms swirled past the right-hand window, attended by the noise of a scuffle.

"Mom!" Gabe shouted, dashing to the window and pressing his face to the cool pane. He noticed the looming outline of the SEAL, and could see part of the driver's side thanks to the diffuse lantern light cast through the glass, but the ground near the tire where his mom had put the bad man was plunged in shadows. "Mom?"

His mother did not respond.

"Mom! Where are you?"

Again there was no answer.

Gabe ran to his father and shook Blade's left shoulder. "Dad, wake up. Mom needs us."

The Warrior's eyelids fluttered briefly.

"Dad! Please wake up!" Gabe urged, shaking even harder. A scream pierced the night outside and Gabe stiffened, petrified. His gaze fell on the Commando, propped against the wall near the door, and he dashed to the Carbine and lifted the weapon awkwardly. If his mother was in danger, he would save her! With that thought uppermost in his mind, Gabe flung open the door and dashed into the night.

He took several steps and halted, thinking of his father alone and unconscious in the cabin, and decided to close the door. As he pulled the door shut a second scream sounded from a dozen yards off, in the direction of the lake. "Mom!" he shouted, and ran around the SEAL.

Vague forms were moving toward the water, and there appeared to be a struggle going on.

Gabe noticed that the figure in the middle had light-colored hair. Blonde hair! "Mom! I'm coming!" he yelled, jogging in pursuit, his left leg bumping against the Commando's magazine.

"No!" Jenny cried. "Go back!"

"I'll save you!" Gabe vowed.

"Go back!"

Gabe raced as fast as he could, but the figures outdistanced him. He received the impression the things were carrying his mother. They came to the lake and, without hesitation, plunged in with a loud splash.

"Gabe! Go—!" Jenny yelled, and was abruptly cut off.

"I'm coming!" Gabe responded, already halfway across the field. He saw two dark forms standing at the edge of the water, but his mother had vanished. "Mom!"

One of the things started toward him.

Stunned, Gabe stopped, his eyes widening, watching the vague figure approach. "Who are you?" he blurted. "What have you done with my mom?"

The thing advanced silently.

Gabe raised the Commando barrel and curled his finger around the trigger. "Who are you?" he repeated, striving to note details. But all he could tell was that the thing stood slightly over five feet in height and possessed a slim body. Was it a person, he wondered, or something else?

The thing hissed.

It wasn't a person, Gabe realized, and he braced himself.

TERROR STRIKE

"Don't come any closer!" he warned. "Just give my mom back."

Ten yards separated them.

"I'll shoot if you don't stop!" Gabe threatened.

Seven yards.

Gabe gulped and wagged the Carbine. "I'm not kidding. Stop or else!"

The thing ignored him.

"What have you done with my mom?" Gabe demanded angrily. He let the figure get closer, to within five yards, and then tensed his arms and squeezed the trigger. The thundering blast of the submachine gun stung his ears as the Commando sent three rounds into the creature. The recoil drove Gabe backwards and he fell onto his backside, still firing.

The powerful bullets lifted the thing from its feet and hurled the creature to the ground in a heap.

Gabe ceased firing and laughed, astonished at his victory. He scrambled erect and stepped tentatively over to the crumpled form. What in the world was it? More importantly, was it dead? He nudged the body with his right foot, and when the thing didn't move he pivoted and took a step toward the lake.

A cold, clammy hand suddenly seized his left wrist.

Startled, Gabe inadvertently screeched and tried to wrench his arm free, but he couldn't tug loose from the viselike hand. He glimpsed the creature he'd shot rising slowly, and he spun to confront it, holding the Commando by his right hand only.

"Let go of me!" he shouted, and fired, able to get off four more rounds before the recoil tore the Commando from his fingers.

The heavy slugs drilled into the creature and slammed it to the earth once again, causing the thing to lose its grip on the boy.

Gabe tottered and stumbled onto his hands and knees. He saw the Carbine clatter to the grass near the creature's legs, and he was about to leap and retrieve the weapon when the thing started to stand.

What *was* it?

He glanced at the lake and spied another creature advancing, and he realized there were too many for him to take on. If he wanted to save his mother, he had to rouse his father at all costs! He straightened and flew toward the cabin, shrieking at the top of his lungs. "Dad! Dad! Help! They've got Mom!"

The cabin seemed so very far away.

Gabe covered five yards and glanced back to see if his pursuers were gaining. His peripheral vision registered something materializing directly in his path, and the next instant he collided with a spongy, yielding body and thin limbs looped about his chest, pinning his arms. He was brusquely lifted from his feet and carted toward the lake.

They had him!

CHAPTER SIXTEEN

"Any last words, jerk?" Harvey asked sarcastically.

Jared extended his arms, palms outward, and took a halting step backward. "Don't!"

"How original," Harvey quipped, and sighted along the arrow.

"No!" Tammy cried.

"What's to stop me?" Harvey cracked.

The answer, spoken in a low tone by the newcomer standing at the edge of the weeds to the south, astounded all of them. "The hand of the Lord."

As one they spun, shocked to behold the massively muscled man in the camouflage clothing who stood there calmly, holding a Bushmaster Auto Pistol in both hands. The firelight illuminated his rugged features and the gash in the center of his forehead. "Drop the bows," he commanded.

"Go to hell!" Harvey snapped.

"You first," the man said, and leveled both Bushmasters and fired.

Harvey and Silas were struck simultaneously. Each was hit

again and again and again, the rounds smacking into their torsos and knocking them backwards. Harvey managed to release his shaft but the arrow went wild. Both men were dead when their bodies thudded onto the ground.

"May the Lord have mercy on their souls," the muscular titan commented.

"Who are you?" Jared blurted.

"My name is Samson. I heard shots and came to investigate."

"You saved our lives," Tammy exclaimed.

Samson scrutinized the bodies littering the clearing, noting the four slain by arrows. "Who are you folks? What are you doing here?"

"I'm Jared, and this is my wife, Tammy," Jared introduced them.

"And this is Betty," Tammy added, nodding at the weeping brunette. "Her husband, Lloyd, was just killed."

"What happened?" Samson inquired.

Jared indicated the two men Samson had shot. "They planned to sell Tammy and Betty to slavers, and they would have succeeded if you hadn't come along."

"You still haven't told me what you're doing here," Samson observed.

"We're waiting for someone," Tammy said.

"A friend," Jared stated. "We can't leave until he returns."

"I'd like to stay and assist you in burying your companions, but I'm in a hurry," Samson mentioned.

"You're leaving already?" Tammy responded. "Why don't you share some food with us?"

Samson walked to the northeast. "I really can't. I'm sorry. Food and rest are out of the question until I've accomplished my mission." He holstered the Auto Pistols.

"Well, we'll be here if you should come by this way again," Jared said. "You're welcome to stop and visit."

"We won't be here if Blade returns first," Tammy mentioned.

TERROR STRIKE

Samson stopped in midstride, then turned. "Blade? Do you know Blade?"

"Yes," Jared answered, and as he studied their rescuer, reflecting that the newcomer was almost as big as Blade and equally as deadly, insight dawned. "You're from the Home, aren't you?"

"Yes," Samson confirmed, "and I'm looking for Blade. When did you see him?"

"He came by here yesterday morning. His wife and son were with him. He promised to pick us up on his return trip in two weeks and take us to the Home."

"Why do you want to go to the Home?"

"We hope to be permitted to live there," Jared said.

"So Blade and his family got this far safely," Samson mused aloud. "Thanks for the information." He went to leave.

"Wait!" Jared declared.

"What?" Samson responded.

"I get the impression Blade and his family are in some kind of danger. He helped us out yesterday and kindly offered to take us to the Home. If he's in trouble, we want to help," Jared offered.

"He might be in trouble," Samson acknowledged, "which is why I must reach him as quickly as I can."

"Let us go with you."

"I'll travel faster alone."

"Please," Jared urged. "We don't want to stay here another two weeks. We don't want to stay another day, if we can help it. Five of us have already been killed. Let us come with you and we'll keep up. I promise. And if Blade is in trouble, we can help."

"Please," Tammy implored, clasping her hands together.

Samson hesitated, torn between his duty and his destire to aid the trio. The pleading expressions on Jared and Tammy convinced him of their sincerity, and the sight of the brunette kneeling over her husband's chest and crying pitiably stirred his compassion. He wanted to let them accompany him, but his wound had slowed him down the last few miles and he couldn't afford to dally.

Jared construed the muscleman's silence as a negative response and became angry. "What's with you people from the Home, anyway? We were told all those wonderful tales about how kind and considerate all of you are, but you don't seem to give a damn about anyone else."

"Jared!" Tammy said, trying to cut him off, afraid he would anger Samson.

"I'm letting him have a piece of my mind!" Jared started testily. "We traveled hundreds of miles to live at the Home, and the first two guys we meet from the Family couldn't care less about our welfare. Blade didn't want his precious trip interrupted, and now this clown is going to go off and leave us without a thought to our safety. We're stuck in the middle of the Outlands, for crying out loud! There's just the three of us left. Our dearest friends are all dead. Is it too much to ask to be taken along so we won't wind up like them?"

Tammy averted her gaze.

"No, it's not too much to ask," Samson said.

"What?" Jared responded in surprise.

"You can come with me, but we must leave immediately," Samson stated. "There's no time to bury your dead."

Hearing that statement, Betty looked up, her eyes moist, tears streaking her cheeks. "I'm not leaving until Lloyd is buried."

Jared began retrieving his revolver and rifle. "We've got to go now, Betty."

"I won't leave Lloyd here to be eaten by animals," Betty said angrily.

"And what about the others?" Tammy chimed in. "We owe it to them to bury them properly."

"We don't have the *time*," Jared insisted.

"Then you go on without me," Betty suggested. "I'll bury my husband and catch up with you."

"You'd never find us in the dark," Tammy said.

Betty shrugged. "If I don't, I don't."

"You wouldn't last ten minutes by yourself," Tammy remarked.

"Without Lloyd, I don't feel much like living anyway," Betty replied softly.

"We can give Lloyd and the others a proper burial tomorrow or the next day," Jared proposed.

"By then the carrior-eaters will have chewed his face down to the bone," Betty said. "I'm not going, and that's final."

"Don't be so stubborn," Jared stated. "Lloyd wouldn't want you to throw your life away needlessly."

Betty folded her arms across her chest and tilted her chin defiantly. "I'm not going."

"Enough!" Samson abruptly commanded and stalked over to them. "This useless arguing is getting us nowhere. I'll compromise this much. Betty, we'll bury your husband right now. But the others will have to wait until after I locate Blade. Is that agreeable with you, Tammy?"

She nodded.

"Okay. Then let's bury Lloyd. With the four of us digging, we can leave in five minutes," Samson said.

Betty, still on her knees, reached out and hugged Samson's legs. "Thank you! Oh, thank you!"

"We'll name our firstborn after you," Jared declared happily, and fell to scooping at the earth with his bare hands.

Samson watched them begin digging, worry gnawing at the back of his mind, hoping he hadn't made a grave error. If the Empaths were right, Blade's life was on the line. And the minutes they now wasted in burying the dead man might well turn out to be the very amount of time that would mean the difference between life and death for Blade. If such turned out to be the case, Samson knew he would never forgive himself.

Which would be small consolation for Blade and his family.

CHAPTER SEVENTEEN

Blade came awake with a start and stared at the ceiling, wondering why he was so cold. He remembered passing out, and he looked down at himself, at the blanket covering him, and knit his brow in bewilderment. Who'd put that there? Jenny? His hands were folded on his chest underneath the blanket, and he raised them so he could see his wound. A flicker of surprise affected him when he laid his eyes on his bandaged midriff. Jenny must have operated already, he realized, and glanced to his left.

The living room was empty.

He gazed at the lantern for a minute, watching the orange flame, and wished he was lying next to the fire. A shiver rippled along his body. He placed his right hand on his hot forehead and licked his dry lips. Evidently, he'd developed a doozy of a fever. A glass of water would be nice.

"Jenny?"

Blade waited patiently for her to reply. He assumed his wife and son were in the bedroom, although he wouldn't have expected them to leave him alone.

"Jenny?" he called out.

He wondered about the time and looked out the west window above the sofa, disconcerted to note that it was pitch black outside and therefore must be the middle of the night. Perhaps Jenny and Gabe were asleep. If Gabe had been afraid to sleep alone, Jenny had probably offered to sleep with him, Blade reasoned. And he didn't want to wake them up.

The Warrior placed his hands flat on the rug and slowly pushed himself to a sitting posture, gritting his teeth as pain lanced his abdomen. He inhaled deeply through his nose and pressed his right forearm to his stomach. Gradually the discomfort subsided and he could breathe easily. He knew Jenny would be furious if he set the wound to bleeding, so he stood carefully, inching upward until he attained his full height, allowing the brown blanket to drop at his feet.

A sticky sweat caked his skin and contributed to his chills. He wiped his left hand on his forehead and took a tentative step. Although he felt extremely weak, he could move without provoking too much agony, and he shuffled to the kitchen counter and reached for the water. His gaze strayed to the open bedroom door.

Blade stiffened.

No one was sleeping in the bed!

"Jenny? Gabe?"

The resultant silence filled the Warrior with dread. Where could they be? he asked himself, and hobbled into the bedroom to check it completely. They wouldn't leave the cabin at night. Jenny knew better. He returned to the living room and stood in the middle of the rug, gripping the straight chair for support, scanning the windows and the door, and made two dismaying observations.

The front door wasn't bolted.

And the Commando and the Beretta were gone.

Blade swallowed hard, shaken by the inescapable conclusion his loved ones had ventured outdoors and not returned. Maybe, he rationalized hopefully, Jenny had just taken Gabe outside to go to the bathroom. For a moment he was relieved, until he realized both lanterns were still in the cabin. Thinking that she might have taken the flashlight, he stepped to the kitchen and rifled through the box of supplies he'd brought inside from the SEAL and deposited on the floor near the cupboard containing the canned goods. He found the flashlight and straightened, holding it in his left palm.

There was no way Jenny would have gone out without a light of some kind.

Unless there'd been an emergency.

Blade slipped the flashlight into his left front pocket and strode to the front door, forgetting all about his wound in his anxiety over his family. He saw the Beeman/Krico leaning on the jamb and grabbed the rifle. The bolt-action rifle wasn't as lethal as the Commando, but it would suffice. He took hold of the doorknob and paused as a cold sensation afflicted him, numbing him momentarily.

The damn chills!

Blade shook his head and opened the door. The cool night air only compounded his condition, and he shivered violently as he stepped from the cabin.

Wait a minute.

What was he doing? Trying to get himself killed?

The Warrior went back into the living room and picked up the lantern off the coffee table. The fever was impairing his mental clarity. If he didn't get his act together, he'd wind up in a world of hurt. The lantern held high, he went out, closed the door, and walked to the front of the SEAL. Not until then did the fact that someone else was missing occur to him.

Where was the lousy scavenger?

Blade's apprehension mounted. What if Roy had revived and kidnapped Jenny and Gabe as a means of getting even? After the beating he'd given the man, Blade would have doubted the scavenger could kidnap a daisy, let alone his wife and son. Maybe Roy was a lot tougher than he'd figured. He opened his mouth to shout Jenny's name, then changed his mind. If Roy was lurking out there somewhere, he certainly didn't want to advertise that he was after the bastard.

Which way should he go?

The Warrior walked toward the lake, swinging the lantern from side to side, straining to distinguish details in the gloom. Another thought struck him, and he halted. The lantern would advertise his presence just as much as a shout would. Roy could undoubtedly spy the light from hundreds of yards off. So what difference did it make if he called out? None.

"Jenny? Gabe? Where are you?"

Blade continued to the south. With his attention focused on the lake shore and the treeline, he almost missed the metallic glint in front of his feet. He glanced down and stopped in amazement.

The Commando!

He hastily slung the Beeman over his left shoulder and scooped up his submachine gun. What was it doing lying in the middle of the field? He sniffed the barrel and frowned. The gun had been fired. A quick check of the magazine confirmed that about ten of the 90 rounds were gone.

Someone had put up a hell of a fight.

Blade headed for the lake, the Commando cradled in his right arm.

"Jenny! Gabe!"

Except for the breeze blowing from the northwest, the night seemed preternaturally still.

The Warrior shuddered again, and guessed that his fever must be worsening. His face felt as if it was on fire. But he refused to rest until he found his wife and son. He would scour the area until he located them or dropped in his tracks.

Tracks.

He came to the lake shore and idly looked at the soft soil, not really expecting to find anything important. So the sight of Jenny's Ruger Blackhawk .44 Magnum lying on the ground stunned him. He knelt, set down the lantern, and examined the revolver. The gun was fully loaded, prompting a slew of questions. Had Jenny lost it? If so, why was she out by the lake? If she hadn't lost the weapon, then who had left it lying there? Surely Roy wouldn't have left it behind. But then, the Beeman hadn't been taken. He sighed in frustration and gazed at the ground.

And saw the print.

Blade blinked a few times and leaned down for a closer inspection. Never before had he beheld such a strange track. Imbedded a quarter of an inch in the earth within inches of the water was a four-toed footprint of bizarre dimensions. Eleven inches in length and three inches wide at the heel, the track was unlike any other he'd ever seen, although it vaguely resembled those of a lizard. The heel was short and rounded and the toes were elongated, comprising eight inches of the total length. The middle pair of toes were two inches longer than those on the inner and outer margins of the foot. Because the track was aligned with the toes pointing due south, he knew whatever had made the print had entered the lake.

But what could it have been?

Strains of inexplicable giantism were not uncommon in the postwar wildlife. The Elders speculated that the radiation was responsible, but they didn't know precisely how the growth spurts in various species were produced. Blade had encountered more than his share of oversized creatures during his travels. In Dallas, Texas, he'd even tangled with a nest of giant lizards. So the print in front of him could conceivably belong to a lizard. Except that most lizards he knew of rarely went into deep water.

What else, then?

Blade gazed out over the lake, endeavoring to piece together the puzzling pieces of the mystery. He debated whether to continue the hunt on foot or in the SEAL. In the shape he was in, he couldn't hike very fast and would tire readily. In the transport he'd be able to conserve his energy and cover more terrain, but he wouldn't be able to penetrate the thicker stands of trees. If he—

A crackling noise sounded to his rear, then abruptly ceased.

TERROR STRIKE 151

The Warrior rotated, the .44 Magnum in his left hand, the Commando in his right. He searched the field but failed to discern a hint of movement. Was his fever inducing his mind to play tricks on him? He doubted it. There was something hiding in the field, observing him. His instincts told him to be wary, that he wasn't alone.

Blade reached back and tucked the .44 Magnum under his belt at the base of his spine. He lifted the lantern in his left hand and walked slowly in the direction of the cabin, his gray eyes flitting from side to side, scanning the weeds. The lantern illuminated a curious greenish-blue hump approximately 20 feet to the west. The hump glistened in the light, as if wet. He angled toward it.

Suddenly the hump uncoiled and darted into the bushes.

Blade glimpsed a long body, a longer tail, and a flurry of slim limbs, and then the thing was gone, vanished in the night. He started toward the bushes, then paused, leery of being led into an ambush. The contours of the creature were disturbingly familiar, but he couldn't identify the thing from his short sighting.

A loud hissing arose to the east, persisted for five seconds, and ended.

As if in response, more hissing sounded to the west, lasted all of ten seconds, and stopped.

Blade hefted the Commando. There must be more than one of the creatures concealed in the field, and they were communicating with one another. He glanced at the SEAL, then at the lake, and froze.

Something was *rising* out of the water near the shore, standing erect on two legs and stepping onto the land.

Blade placed the lantern at his feet and pressed the Commando to his right shoulder.

Another figure began rising out of the lake, then another, and yet another.

The Warrior rested his finger on the trigger and disregarded the chilly feeling intensifying in his body. At last he knew what had happened to his wife and son. The creatures had gotten them. And if Jenny and Gabe had been pulled under the water, they were udoubtedly dead by now. The notion aroused a burning rage, and he sneered as he sighted on the foremost thing and fired a short, controlled burst.

Suddenly creatures popped up all over the field.

Blade saw his initial target topple backwards, and he swiveled and pointed the barrel at a five-foot-tall form that had risen in a clump of weeds ten feet to the right. He sent a half-dozen rounds into the thing's torso and it fell from view. But there were many more, on all sides, and some hissed as they converged on him.

What *were* they?

He was about to shoot at a second creature when the one he'd just fired at reappeared, standing in the same spot as before. For an instant he believed it was a different creature, until it doubled over, apparently injured and holding its arms to its chest, and lumbered straight at him.

The thing had taken direct hits in the chest and survived!

Blade elevated the barrel slightly, going for the head this time, and let the creature have six more bullets. The impact flipped the figure into the bushes, and Blade grinned in triumph. Their heads were their weak spots!

A twig snapped to his rear.

The Warrior whirled, his cockiness replaced by openmouthed consternation when he saw one of the beings less than two yards from him. In the second before he squeezed the trigger, Blade clearly saw its features: a rounded, blunt head notable for a pair of widely separated, bulbous black eyes and a slit of a mouth; moist, smooth, greenish-blue skin; a slender body lacking shoulders and hips; thin limbs, the lower longer than the upper; four extended digits at the end of its "arms", five at the end of its "legs"; and a long, flat tail that helped support the creature as it walked erect. Like the rest, this one stood about five feet in height.

Blade fired, and he saw the slugs tear into the thing's head

TERROR STRIKE 153

and knock it to the ground. He watched it thrash and convulse for a moment, at last confirming what he was up against.

Mutations.

Once, perhaps a century ago, their ancestors had been insignificant salamanders, secretive and nocturnal amphibians equally at home on land or in the water. Once, before the staggering amount of radiation and chemical toxins were unleashed on the environment, the ancestors of these creatures had roamed the woods at night seeking prey. All salamanders were carnivorous.

And there were no exceptions.

There wasn't time for Blade to dwell on the factors contributing to the creation of the giant mutant strain. There wasn't time to reflect upon the irony of humankind's superweapons transforming nature itself into an adversary. There was only time for firing and downing as many as he could.

Blade tried his utmost. He swept the Commando in an arc, blasting four of the salamanders coming at him from the west. Spinning, he sent a hail of lead into three approaching from the east.

Something abruptly grabbed him about the ankles.

Blade looked down and found a salamander on all fours, holding fast to his legs and striving to jerk him off balance. He rammed the barrel into the creature's left eye and fired, the rounds rupturing the orb and the cranium and spraying gore all over his fatigue pants.

The salamander slumped to the earth lifeless.

The Warrior realized they could travel on all fours as well as on two legs, and he stared toward the lake and spied one doing just that, scuttling at him with the speed of a streaking snake. He stitched the thing from head to tail, flipping the creature onto its back.

Many others closed in on him.

Blade downed three more when the inevitable occurred; the Commando went empty.

A salamander charged him, running manlike.

Blade reversed his grip on the submachine gun and swung it as a club, slamming the stock into the salamander's mouth and catapulting it onto the ground. He reached behind his back and drew the .44 Magnum, aimed, and flattened another foe.

Still they came on.

He heard a twig snap and whirled to catch a pair of mutations less than six feet away. Two quick shots killed them both, the .44 Magnum booming.

They surrounded him now.

Blade fired a final time, slaying an onrushing salamander. Two others darted in from different directions, running on all fours, keeping their bodies level with the ground. He attempted to get a bead on one of them, but they moved too rapidly. Only when the pair were almost to him did he perceive that he wasn't their target.

They were after the lantern!

The Warrior tried to lunge and grab the lantern before they could reach it, but the speedier of the duo hit the lantern without breaking stride, using its blunt head to deliver a smashing blow. Tumbling crazily, the lantern went sailing.

The flame went out.

Darkness engulfed Blade. He squinted, endeavoring to locate the salamanders, but he needn't have bothered.

They knew where he was and they came to him.

The mutations hurled themselves at the Warrior, springing at him from every direction at once, seven, eight, ten of them working in concert. More piled on, seeking to overwhelm him by sheer force of numbers.

Blade was driven to his knees by the weight of their bodies. He struck at them, punching with his left hand and clubbing them with the barrel of the Blackhawk, swinging right and left in reckless abandon. They hit him on his head and shoulders and tried to grab his arms. He held his own briefly, until he released the Ruger and tried to draw his right Bowie, leaving his right side exposed.

The hissing salamanders swarmed over the Warrior, burying

him in their moist, writhing flesh. Four of them locked their limbs on his right arm. Three others succeeded in clamping their arms around his neck. His legs were yanked out from under him.

Blade came down hard on his stomach. A pervading weakness brought on by his exertion, his fever, and his wound caused him to go briefly limp. Before he could recover, they seized his arms and legs in unbreakable holds and, en masse, lifted him into the air.

They had won.

CHAPTER EIGHTEEN

Blade felt them carrying him, felt their cool digits on his arms and shoulders and face. He was too disoriented, too tired and sore, to pay much attention to where they were taking him. Waves of vertigo tried to swamp him, but he fought them off, forcing himself to stay awake. His mind seemed sluggish. For a minute the issue was in doubt, and he came close to passing out. But just when he thought he would slip into unconsciousness, the salamanders revived him.

They carried him into the lake.

He heard the splashing as the creatures entered the water, and the sound sent a current of shock through him. They planned to drown him, to consume him underwater! Jenny and Gabe must have suffered the same fate! His fury returned, and the resultant adrenaline surge restored his full alertness and imbued him with newfound strength. "No!" he bellowed, and attempted to tear his arms and legs from their collective grasp.

The salamanders paused to tighten their grips.

Blade bucked and heaved, jerking this way and that, his muscles bulging, sweat pouring from his skin. He exerted his

TERROR STRIKE

might to the maximum, ignoring the agony in his abdomen, but there were too many for him.

Moving methodically, the mutations marched into the lake.

The icy water touched Blade's legs first, soaking his pants, then drenched his back and began to rise over his chest. He endeavored to slow them down by rocking from side to side, but the creatures were undeterred.

Blade gasped as the frigid water crept higher and higher. Despair welled within him. If he was going to die, he preferred to go out fighting, or else expire of old age in his bed with his wife at his side. To be helplessly drowned by horrid mutations seemed an ignoble manner of dying.

The water lapped against his chin.

Blade instinctively held his breath, drawing as much air as he could into his lungs. The cold water invigorated him and made his skin tingle. His despair gave way to hope. Maybe, once they were underwater, he could break free. The water was bound to make him slippery to hold.

Lowering smoothly into the lake, the salamanders submerged completely and swam into deeper water. They angled toward the west shore, swimming powerfully, using their hind legs and tails to propel them.

The Warrior struggled for only a few seconds and realized their grip on him was as strong as ever. He conserved his energy, waiting for them to release him and begin their feeding frenzy, envisioning them attacking him as if they were a school of firece piranha. Instead, to his growing astonishment, they appeared to be in a hurry to reach a particular destination, not to rip him to shreds.

What were they doing?

His chest started to ache and he wondered how long he could hold his breath. Two minutes? Three? Four? He hadn't done any swimming on a regular basis in years and was badly out of practice. Except for an occasional dip in the moat during which he would dive down and touch the bottom, he'd rarely had any reason to hold his breath.

He definitely had a reason now.

Blade peered ahead, trying to spot their destination, but the murky water restricted his field of vision to within a yard of his face, and even then he could only perceive dim outlines. The surface of the lake, however, was visible as a lighter mantle of gray against the backdrop of the night.

The salamanders increased their speed.

Blade grimaced as the gnawing ache in his chest became general torment. His fever flared terribly. He perceived an enormous dark mass materializing in front of them and deduced they were rapidly nearing the west bank.

Were the mutations intending to climb out of the lake again?

The Warrior anticipated them arching upward, but they swam on a beeline for the bank without slowing or deviating their course. His cheeks puffed out and his throat felt as if the pressure threatened to cause him to explode.

A black cavity abruptly loomed in the west bank. The salamanders glided into the opening and kicked harder.

Blade had the impression he was rising, and to his amazement he unexpectedly burst from the water and felt dank air on his face. He automatically inhaled, his chest expanding, overcome with relief. The creatures had brought him to their lair, some sort of underground cavern! He was lifted and pulled and shoved, then dumped unceremoniously onto soft earth. The lair was pitch black, but he didn't care.

They'd released him!

And he still lived! Not only that, he still had his Bowies!

A smile twisted his features and he rose to his knees. A series of splashes arose nearby and he surmised the creatures were returning to the lake. After a bit the lair became eerily quiet. Blade ran his hands through his soaked hair and coughed.

"What was that?" a youthful voice asked.

"Quiet," responded a woman who Blade knew better than any other on the planet.

The Warrior felt as if a lightning bolt had jolted his body. He swung in the direction of the voices and experienced difficulty in finding his own. "Jenny! Gabe!" he finally blurted

TERROR STRIKE

out. Their answering cries were literally music to his ears.

"Daddy!"

"Blade?"

"Stay where you are!" Blade told them. He judged his loved ones to be very close, within ten feet of his position, but he didn't want to fumble hastily toward them in the darkness and fall into the water. His left hand closed on his left pocket and found the flashlight still there. "I have a light," he said, and pulled the flashlight from his pocket. Would the thing still work, he fretted, after being submerged? Trembling as much from his excitement as from the chills, he pressed the button.

The thin beam of light played over Jenny and Gabe, who were huddled together eight feet off. Gabe impetuously let go of his mom and scrambled on his hands and knees across the mud floor toward his father. Jenny followed.

Blade took them into his arms and hugged them tight, bowing his head in thankfulness. A constriction in his throat prevented him from speaking until he swallowed and said huskily, "I didn't think I'd ever see either of you again."

Soft sniffles came from Gabe.

Jenny kissed Blade tenderly on the lips.

Although the Warrior wanted to prolong their reunion and embrace them indefinitely, he knew better. Time was precious. The mutations might return at any second. For all he knew, there could be a few lurking nearby. The thought prompted him to move his left hand back and forth and up and down, flicking the flashlight beam around the lair, gauging its dimensions.

The salamander's subterranean abode consisted of an earthen excavation 30 feet wide and slightly under six feet in height. The walls and ceiling were compact dirt, but the floor had been turned to mud by the constant dripping of the creatures. A circular pool of water ten feet in diameter linked the lair to the lake.

Blade spied whitish objects in the far corner and swiveled the flashlight to illuminate them. He almost recoiled when he saw the piles of bones littering the floor. Among the grisly collection were two human skeletons.

"I knew you'd come save us," Gabe commented happily.

"Yeah. What kept you so long?" Jenny quipped, and laid her moist cheek on his.

"You forgot to leave a note telling me you'd gone to visit the neighbors," Blade replied. He kissed her, then released them.

"What do we do now?" Gabe asked.

"We get out of here," Blade said, and patted his right Bowie.

"Take me too," interjected a weak, raspy voice to his rear.

The Warrior swung around and trained the flashlight on the person he discovered lying in the opposite corner from the bones. "Roy!" he blurted out.

"Help me," the scavenger responded. He lay on his back, his wrists and ankles bound, his visage a battered ruin, mud coating his clothing. "Please help me!"

"He wanted me to untie him, but I wouldn't," Jenny said.

"How'd he know you were in here?" Blade asked.

"Those terrible things brought him down first, then me. When they dropped me on the ground I didn't know where I was. I sat in the dark and tried to figure out what to do next. Then they brought Gabe in and I heard him coughing and calling for me. We crawled to each other. That's when the pervert opened his mouth and asked me to untie him," Jenny detailed.

"Please, mister!" Roy begged. "Don't let those things eat me."

"Let them, Dad," Gabe said.

"He deserves whatever happens to him," Jenny concurred.

Blade glanced at them, their features cast in shadows. "I never realized the two of you were so bloodthirsty."

"Do you expect us to show mercy to him after what he did to us?" Jenny countered.

"Yeah. He's scum," Gabe added.

TERROR STRIKE

The Warrior sighed and extended the flashlight to Jenny. "Here. Take this."

"What are you planning to do?" she inquired as she took it.

"I'm going to cut him loose," Blade said.

"What?" Jenny queried in disbelief.

"I'm going to cut him loose," Blade reiterated.

"But *why*?"

"Because no matter what he's done—and I'd kill him in a second for the pain he inflicted on us if we weren't in here—he's human."

"So was Jack the Ripper."

Blade rose to a crouch. "Jenny, I can't just leave him there to be eaten by the mutations. I'm a Warrior, not a psychopath. I'll free him and then he's on his own."

"Let me get this straight. You'll cut him loose so the mutants won't eat him, but if you bump into him after we're out of here, you'll kill him?"

"Exactly."

Jenny made a snorting sound and muttered, "Men!"

Blade took a partial step forward, doubled over at the waist, when he heard the water lapping against the edge of the pool and sensed a commotion in the water. "Douse the flashlight!" he directed, and quickly took Jenny and Gabe protectively into his arms.

Blackness enveloped the lair once again.

The Warrior listened to splashing noises, then the muffled tread of something shuffling across the floor. He detected a hint of movement, and conjectured that one of the creatures had returned. His supposition was confirmed moments later when the scavenger uttered a harsh exclamation.

"Get your slimy paws off me!"

Blade could feel the tension in Jenny and Gabe, and he wondered if they could feel his.

"Let go of me!" Roy bellowed.

The Warrior placed his hands on the hilts of his knives.

"Damn you! Let go! What—!" Roy cried, and vented a

strangled, gurgling gasp.

Blade leaned closer to his wife. "When I give you the word, shine the flashlight over there."

"Got it," she said.

A peculiar, squishy, ripping noise arose in the corner, then a spattering noise, as if a liquid substance was spraying over the floor.

Blade realized what had happened and knew he'd waited too long, but he hadn't expected the things to finish Roy off so quickly. He drew the Bowies, whispered, "Now!" and dashed toward the corner as Jenny turned on the flashlight.

The beam revealed a gory tableau. Three mutations were gathered around the scavenger's body. Roy was dead, his head torn from his body, blood spurting from his severed neck. One of the salamanders held Roy's head in its left hand while it gnawed on the jagged stump under Roy's chin. The second creature lapped at the crimson geyser sprinkling the floor, and the third was in the act of stripping off the scavenger's clothes. The sudden illumination made them whirl toward the source. They dropped whatever they were doing and raised their hands to shield their bulging eyes.

Blade plowed into them at an awkward run, his speed impaired by his having to run stooped over. He felt the ceiling scraping his broad shoulders and wished he could straighten to his full stature, but he would have to make do, and make do he did. His left forearm batted the foremost salamander backwards, and the thing tripped over the scavenger's corpse and toppled to the ground. Blade arced the right Bowie out and around, and the keen razor edge slit the second creature's throat from one side to the other. A putrid fluid spurted out. The creature clutched at its neck and sank to its knees. Blade kicked it in the face, and his combat boot sent the thing crashing into the wall.

The third mutation hissed and lunged.

The Warrior met the lunge with both Bowies leveled, impaling the creature in the area of its body where its chest would be if the thing had a chest. He surged his arms upward, cracking the mutation's head on the compact dirt ceiling, then brutally flung the salamander to the right.

Limp as a wet rag, the creature slipped off the Bowies and fell.

Leaving the one Blade had struck with his arm.

The Warrior saw the thing come up and over Roy's body in a savage rush. He tried a new tactic, swinging the Bowies out and in, hacking at the mutation's eyes.

Displaying astounding reflexes, the salamander raised both upper limbs to block the knives. Instead, the Bowies cleaved through both arms. chopping the hands off. The hands plopped into the mud and continued to open and close, even though detached. The creature's lifeblood gushed out the sundered wrists.

Blade sank his left Bowie into the salamander's head between its eyes. He wrenched the knife free and watched the mutation keel over. All three were now on the ground, and only the one with the slit throat still moved, twitching and convulsing, its movements weaker and weaker with each passing second.

"You did it!" Gabe shouted.

"Not so loud," Blade advised. He wiped the Bowies on his pants and returned to his wife and son.

"More of those things may show up at any minute," Jenny noted.

"I know," Blade said, "which is why we're leaving right this instant. Are you both up to another swim?"

Gabe glanced at the pool apprehensively. "I had a hard time holding my breath the first time, Dad."

"Don't worry. We'll swim as fast as we can. And once we're out of the lair and in the lake, we'll swim straight up to the surface. If my calculations are correct, we'll be within yards of the western shore. You won't need to swim as far this time," Blade assured him.

"There are dozens more out there somewhere," Jenny remarked. "Even if we make it out of the lake, what do we do then? Try and take shelter in the cabin? They could break in there easy enough."

"I doubt they know how to open a door or a window. If they did, they would have broken in on us last night."

"Or during the day," Gabe commented.

"Did you see the way they reacted to the flashlight?" Blade asked, and went on before his son could answer. "I suspect they're nocturnal."

"What's nocturnal?" Gabe queried.

"They're only abroad at night. Bright sunlight is probably too hard on their sensitive eyes."

"Oh."

Jenny gestured at the pool. "So what do we do once we're out? Hide in the forest until dawn?"

"No. They might be able to track by scent, and we already know their eyesight at night is exceptional. I also don't much like the idea of taking shelter in the cabin. Sooner or later they'll figure out how to get inside."

"Then what do we do?" Jenny inquired.

"Our best bet is to reach the SEAL. Once we're inside the transport, we'll be safe. There's no way those things can break into the van."

"But the field will be swarming with them," Jenny noted. "They'll be all over the area, hunting for food."

"I know," Blade said. "They must scour the woods in the vicinity of the lake for game during the night, and bring the animals they catch down here to store until they're ready to eat."

"Maybe those three who killed the bad man had the munchies," Gabe mentioned, and laughed.

"Remind me to have a talk with you about your sense of humor, young man, after we return to the Home," Jenny stated.

Blade was pleased that they could banter in the midst of such a crisis. The Elder who taught the novice Warriors their trade never tired of stressing the fundamental importance of attitude in a life-threatening situation. Attitude ranked as high as ability and an aptitude for dispensing death. With a positive attitude, a person could face insurmountable odds and triumph or could observe the most sickening violence and retain his or her self-control. Without a positive attitude, the barbarism the Warriors confronted would ravage them emotionally.

"I'm ready when you are, Dad," Gabe declared.

"Okay. I'll hold onto you and your mom will stay by our side," Blade said. He looked at Jenny. "If you want, I'll hold your hand until we're clear of the lair."

"I want."

"Then let's go."

CHAPTER NINETEEN

Samson, Jared, Tammy, and Betty emerged from the forest bordering the southwest curve of the lake and halted.

"What was all that shooting we heard earlier?" Tammy asked.

"I don't know," Samson replied. He didn't bother to add that the gunfire had worried him immensely. He'd engaged in numerous target-practice sessions with Blade at the shooting range in the southeast corner of the Home, and he knew the distinctive, heavy thundering of the Commando Arms Carbine well. The gunfire he'd heard had included bursts from a Commando.

"What's that light?" Jared questioned, staring to the north.

The Warrior pivoted and spied the dim glow at the north end of the lake. According to the information imparted by Plato, the Founder's cabin was located near the north shore. "That's where we're headed," he announced, and moved off.

Jared kept pace on Samson's right while the women trailed behind.

"It seems peaceful here," Betty remarked.

"Appearances can be deceiving," the Warrior said.

"Do you think Blade will be mad that we came along?" Jared inquired.

"No. Why should he?" Samson responded, his attention on the distant light. He held the Bushmaster Auto Rifle in his right hand.

"I don't know. But I got the impression he's not the kind of guy you'd want to tick off."

"He's not," Samson confirmed.

"I also get the impression he's an important person at the Home."

"You certainly get a lot of impressions. Yes, he is."

"In what way?"

"There are eighteen Family members who have been chosen by the Elders to serve as Warriors, as the guardians of the Home. Blade is the head Warrior," Samson elaborated. "The only one who has more authority than Blade is our Leader, and even then only in times of peace. In times of war Blade is in command."

Jared studied the muscular figure next to him. "And you must be one of the Warriors, huh?"

"Yes."

"Do you mind if I ask you something?"

"Heaven forbid."

"What?"

"Never mind. Go ahead. Ask."

Jared cleared his throat. "Are all the men at the Home as big as Blade and you are?"

Samson glanced at his newfound companion, trying to read Jared's expression in the dark. "No."

"Whew! I was beginning to think that all men in the Family are giants and I'd be a midget in comparison."

"No, we're not all giants," Samson said, suppressing an urge to laugh.

"Thank goodness."

"Actually, Blade and I are the runts in the Family."

There was a pregnant pause, and then came Jared's sheepish

response. "You're kidding, right?"

Samson suddenly halted and turned to scan the inky vegetation ten yards to his left. "Listen," he said softly.

Jared cocked his head. "I don't hear anything."

"Neither do I," Samson stated.

"So?"

"So what happened to the insects?"

"The insects?" Jared repeated, and abruptly comprehended. Moments before the forest had been alive with the buzzing and chirping of countless bugs. Now the woods were like a tomb. Even the breeze had abated.

"What does it mean?" Tammy whispered.

"Stay alert," Samson warned, cradling the Bushmaster against his right side.

"You don't have to tell me twice," Tammy said nervously.

The Warrior looked at the brunette. She had spoken only a few times since her husband's burial, and then only when addressed. Her countenance was pale. On several occasions Samson had had to remind her not to fall too far behind the rest as they'd hastened toward the lake. He recognized her symptoms from previous experience. The poor woman suffered from delayed-stress syndrome, as the Elder who'd taught Combat Psychology 101 had described the condition. Anyone who lived through a harrowing ordeal could succumb to a belated reaction when the full shock set in. The trauma of losing Lloyd was almost more than Betty could bear. "How about you? Are you okay?"

"Never felt better," Betty answered caustically.

"I'm serious."

"So am I," she said, and laughed lightly. "Why shouldn't I be okay? Just because I lost the man I loved today? Or because life in this stinking world sucks?" She paused, then launched into a bitter tirade. "I mean, what's the reason we're here? Why are we put on this rotten world to suffer? From the cradle to the grave all we know is pain. Everywhere you turn there's violence and death. If the raiders, the murderers, the robbers, the mutations, the animals, or some disease doesn't get you, it's a miracle. All Lloyd and I wanted out of a life was a peaceful place to raise our children, a place where we wouldn't have to worry about being attacked every time we stepped out the door. A place where men and women treat each other with mutual respect. A place where everyone trusts everyone else."

"Put your trust in the Lord."

Betty snickered. "Now I *know* you're not serious."

"But I am. Without faith and trust in the Lord, life is a sham."

"How do you figure?"

Samson gazed at the trees and frowned. "This isn't the proper time or place to discuss this. How about if we continue our conversation later?"

Betty's chin drooped to her chest. "Yeah. Sure. Later," she replied, her words barely audible.

"I'm sorry," Samson told her.

She motioned for him to keep going.

The Warrior regretfully turned his back on her and hiked northward. The silence still shrouded the woods, signifying that someone or something had disrupted the natural rhythm of the wildlife. He wished the Empaths could have been more specific about the nature of the threat to Blade. To be forewarned was to be forearmed, he'd always believed.

A loud splash sounded in the lake.

"Hey, maybe we can have fish for breakfast," Jared commented.

"How can you think about food at a time like this?" Tammy asked.

"It's easy. I didn't have supper."

"No more talking," Samson ordered, staring across the placid water. He wasn't very surprised when one of them ignored him.

"Can I have a drink before we go any farther?" Betty queried.

"It can wait," Samson said.

"Please. I don't feel so good."

The Warrior pursed his lips. If he refused, she might be miffed and would be of even less value in a fight. He pointed at the lake. "Splash some water on your face, but don't drink it."

"Why not?"

"The water might be contaminated."

Betty stepped to the edge of the lake and knelt on her right knee. She extended her right arm and cupped a cool handful, and she was about to raise her arm when a thin form broke the murky surface, hurtling at her with its limbs outstretched, hissing loudly. Her sluggish mind betrayed her. The thing was almost upon her before she could do more than blink. It was that quick.

But not quick enough.

Samson's Auto Rifle chattered when the creature was less than 12 inches from its prey. The rounds smacked into its torso and propelled it backwards into the lake, where the thing promptly sank from view.

"Dear God!" Tammy exclaimed. She moved to Betty's side and assisted the stunned woman in rising.

"What was that?" Jared asked anxiously.

"Your guess is as good as mine," Samson replied, and walked over to the women. "Are you all right, Betty?" he inquired.

She nodded absently. "Yeah. Yeah. Sure."

"We can't stop. We have to reach the light at the end of the lake. Can you keep up with us?"

"Yeah. Yeah."

"I'll take care of her," Tammy offered.

"Be ready for anything," Samson advised them. He hurried in the direction of the cabin, certain their troubles had just begun. The creature in the water had appeared to be manlike, but he'd glimpsed it for only a few seconds. Since no known animal resembled what he'd seen, he concluded the thing must

TERROR STRIKE   171

have been a mutation. And where there was one mutant, there invariably were more. Was that the threat? Were there mutants in the lake? "Don't stray near the water," he recommended.

"You don't have to tell me twice," Jared whispered.

The Warrior studied the light ahead, puzzled. There seemed to be a large, squarish object, a boulder perhaps, interposed between the light and the lake. A faint halo outlined a portion of the object.

A twig snapped to his left.

Samson scrutinized the trees, pondering. The insects wouldn't have ceased droning unless there was something in the forest. The things in the lake wouldn't bother the insects at all. Unless, of course, the creatures in the lake were also in the forest. Or, conceivably, there might be two menaces, one in the water, the other skulking in the woods. Which meant walking along the shore qualified as being caught between the proverbial rock and a hard place. But he had no choice. He'd already wasted too much time. It was imperative he find Blade right away.

They proceeded along the western shore until they were 40 yards from the indistinct glow.

"I saw something," Betty unexpectedly declared.

Samson stopped and glanced at her. "Where?"

"In the trees," Betty replied. "I don't know what it was."

Samson wondered if her overwrought nerves explained her sighting. He decided to give her the benefit of the doubt. "If you see anything else, let me know."

"Will do."

The Warrior hiked faster. He wasn't about to dispute her and cause her to regress when she was beginning to snap out of her befuddled state. The incident with the creature must have startled her enough to bring her back to her senses.

In short order they came to a field.

His eyes narrowing in perplexity, Samson studied the odd object now 20 yards distant, bothered by a feeling he should know what it was. And in five strides he did.

It was the SEAL.

How could he have been so stupid? Samson asked himself. He knew Blade had driven to the lake in the transport. Visible above and beyond the vehicle was the Founder's cabin, a sturdy log structure, the front faintly illuminated by a light source inside that streamed through the windows and reflected off the SEAL.

Samson slowed, extra wary now. There was no hint of movement within the cabin. There weren't any shadows playing across the glass panes. And he doubted that Blade's family would have retired so early.

The Nazarite dreaded to open the door. He feared the worst, feared that the delays had prevented him from reaching the scene in time to save his friend. With the Bushmaster Auto Rifle leveled, he approached the cabin, skirting the front end of the SEAL. He tried the transport's door, which turned out to be locked.

"Keep watch," Samson commanded the others.

"You want us to stay out here?" Jared whispered in response.

"Yes."

"I was afraid you'd say that," Jared muttered.

Samson tested the doorknob, and was surprised to discover it unlocked. He twisted the knob and shoved, leaning against the jamb as the door opened. "Blade?" he called. "Jenny? Gabe? Are you here?" When no reply was forthcoming, he glided across the living room to a kitchenette, then gazed into a neat bedroom. The cabin was vacant. He noticed a livingroom window had been completely shattered. He glanced at the flickering lantern, debating his next move.

Jared suddenly cried out frantically. "Samson! Get out here!"

The Warrior grabbed the lantern by the handle and dashed outside to find the three of them standing near the transport's grill and staring into the field. "What is it?" he asked, joining them.

TERROR STRIKE

Jared appeared to be almost in shock. He simply nodded. Samson faced the field and felt his skin crawl.

Dozens of greenish-blue horrors with bulbous eyes and long tails were converging on the cabin, advancing slowly, walking erect. Those in the foremost ranks raised their hands over their eyes as the lantern light bathed them.

"What are they?" Tammy asked needlessly of no one in particular, her voice wavering fearfully.

"Mutants," Samson said, scrutinizing the creatures closely. "Amphibians of some sort would be my guess." The things were 15 feet off. He elevated the lantern for a better look.

And a strange thing happened.

The nearest creatures stopped and twisted their heads away from the light, then came on again walking sideways.

"They don't like the light," Samson instantly deduced.

"Let's set the cabin on fire," Jared suggested.

"Be serious," Samson admonished him.

"I was."

"What do you think they want?" Betty asked in a hushed, dazed tone.

"That should be obvious," Tammy said.

"What do we do?" Jared inquired, sounding petrified.

"We call on the Lord for deliverance," Samson stated calmly.

Betty unexpectedly tittered inanely. "While we're at it, why don't we call on the Tooth Fairy? God doesn't care if we live or die. God doesn't care if we suffer."

"You're wrong," Samson said, his eyes on the amphibians.

"Am I? Look at what happened to Lloyd!" Betty snapped, her tone brittle. "Why didn't God save him? Why didn't God spare me the anguish of a life without my husband? I'll tell you why!"

Samson fingered the trigger on his Auto Rifle, trying to concentrate on the tightening ring of mutations. Their appearance had evidently set Betty off again. She needed attention, needed comforting, but he couldn't allow himself to be distracted when they were about to be attacked.

"Better yet, I'll show you!" Betty cried, her voice breaking.

Before Samson or the others could stop her, Betty walked rapidly toward the mutations.

"Betty!" Tammy shouted. "Don't!"

Samson went after her, but he took only a few strides before Betty glanced over her left shoulder, saw him coming, and ran up to the nearest amphibian.

"Betty!" Jared yelled.

The Warrior started to step to the right. He wanted a clear shot at the mutation, which stood within two feet of Betty, its body sideways, staring at her through its spread fingers. "Betty, get back here," he ordered.

"No!" Betty responded. "I'll show you. I'll prove I'm right." She held her rifle level at her waist. Slowly, smiling all the while, she lowered the barrel and extended her right hand to the creature in a friendly gesture. "Hi," she said. "We don't want to harm you."

"Don't!" Tammy exclaimed.

For several breathless seconds nothing happened. The mutations had halted and were watching their fellow, who stood stock still and regarded Betty coldly.

Samson took another cautious stride. Another few inches and he would be able to get off a shot.

Laughing lightly, Betty looked back. "Well, what do you know. I guess I was wrong."

The creature was on her in the twinkling of an eye, its hands clamping on the sides of her head and twisting.

They all heard her spine snap.

"No!" Samson roared, and took three full steps. He squeezed the trigger, gripping the weapon firmly in his right hand to absorb the recoil, and sent six rounds into the lead mutant. The slugs doubled it in half, the impact tearing the thing away from Betty and flinging it to the earth.

Without the amphibian's arms to support her, Betty sank down, her eyes gazing lifelessly at the stars.

Jared and Tammy opened up, their rifles booming.

The Warrior backpedaled, sweeping the Auto Rifle in a half circle, firing a sustained burst. The high-velocity bullets punctured torso after torso, flinging seven of the abominations into the weeds.

Hissing in concert, the rest of the mutations charged. A few dropped to all fours and skittered forward lizard like.

Samson saw an onrushing amphibian, its body held low to the ground, streaking toward him out of the night. He aimed the Bushmaster, leading the creature by a few yards, and fired. The rounds hit the thing in the head and flipped it over.

On all sides the mutations were steadily advancing.

Jared and Tammy expended the ammunition in their rifles and drew their revolvers.

The Warrior came to the front of the SEAL and motioned with the lantern at the cabin. "Inside! Get indoors! We stand a better chance in there!"

They hastily retreated into the cabin and Jared slammed the door shut. "Now what?" he asked. "They have us trapped in here."

"But they can't all get to us at once," Samson said, moving to the counter and depositing the lantern.

"Look!" Tammy cried.

Amphibian faces were peering in at every window, including the open livingroom window, dozens of them, regarding the humans balefully, their mouths thin slits.

"They give me the creeps," Jared muttered. He threw the bolt on the door. "Mutants always do."

"Maybe they won't come in," Tammy said hopefully.

"Reload your rifles," Samson directed them, and stepped to the bedroom doorway. He saw more mutations staring in at the bedroom window.

The cabin was completely surrounded.

"What's that vehicle outside?" Jared asked while feeding cartridges into his Marlin.

"It's called the SEAL. Blade drove it to the lake," Samson

answered.

"Any chance of us getting inside and driving off?"

"No," Samson replied. He began refilling the Auto Rifle's magazine, working swiftly.

"Why not?"

"I don't have the keys," Samson said, his fingers flying.

"Figures," Jared declared. "The way our luck has been running, I'm surprised those things don't try and come in."

A resounding crash came from the bedroom.

Samson whirled, his features hardening at the sight of a mutant using a tree limb to smash the glass out of the bedroom window. He slapped the full magazine into the Bushmaster, took four steps into the room, and let the amphibians framed by the window have it, pouring a withering hail of lead into their bodies.

The creatures jerked and thrashed as they were struck, and four of them dropped on the spot, one sprawling over the windowsill, his arms dangling down.

More crashing arose in the living room, the sound of glass breaking and tinkling to the floor. Then gunshots.

"Samson!" Tammy screamed.

The Warrior darted to the doorway, dreading the worst and confirming his fear.

Amphibians had broken the remaining living room window and were through all the windows attempting to clamber inside, hissing vociferously, as if they were a nest of vipers. Other mutations were battering on the front door.

Jared and Tammy were shooting as fast as they could, but there were too many windows to cover, too many creatures outside pressing to get it, for them to stop them all.

Samson aimed at the west window, at a mutation perched on the sill and about to jump to the floor, and fired from the hip. His rounds slammed into the creature's head and neck and hurtled it into its comrades outside. A thumping noise behind him made the Warrior spin, and there were two amphibians already in the bedroom and springing toward him with their maws wide. He cut loose at almost point-blank range, his slugs nearly tearing them in half.

More were coming in the bedroom window.

A pair of the creatures vaulted through the west window.

And the front door suddenly snapped from its hinges and tilted at a steep angle for a moment before thudding onto the rug, narrowly missing Jared and Tammy.

The amphibians poured into the cabin.

CHAPTER TWENTY

Blade spied the gray expanse of the surface 15 feet above him, arched his back, and kicked his legs furiously, pumping with all his strength. He could feel Gabe's arms around his neck and the tension in his son's body. The fingers of his right hand were interlaced with Jenny's left hand. He flicked his eyes right and left, on the lookout for the salamanders. If the mutations assaulted them now, when they were in the open, underwater, and he had his hands full, their escape would be doomed. They were vulnerable in the water.

A dark form materialized a few feet above him.

Blade stiffened and slowed, prepared to give his own life, if necessary, so his loved ones could flee. But his sacrifice wasn't needed; the form belonged to a large fish. He watched it swim lazily to the east, then resumed his ascent.

Where were the salamanders?

He broke the surface seconds later and gasped, then lifted Gabe out of the water and hauled on Jenny's arm, adding the power in his arm to her momentum so she could reach the surface that much sooner. Her head and shoulders shot out

TERROR STRIKE

of the lake and she breathed in the cool night air noisily.

Gabe coughed and clung to his father.

"We did it!" Jenny said, elated.

"But we're not out of the woods yet," Blade reminded her. He glanced at the rather steep bank rimming the water at that point, less than ten feet away, and paddled toward land.

Jenny released his hand and swam alongside him. "Are you okay, Gabe?" she asked.

"Yep," the boy replied, then added, "What's all that noise?"

Blade heard the sounds too, the unmistakable blasting of gunfire, an automatic and rifles firing repeatedly. To his amazement, the gunfire seemed to be coming from the direction of the cabin.

"What's going on?" Jenny queried.

"I don't know," Blade told her. He came to the bank and halted, debating whether to try and scale the embankment or to swim to the north where the ground formed the level shoreline he'd fished from. Since he was averse to remaining in the water any longer than was absolutely essential, he opted to climb the bank.

A stout bush, its silhouette an inky outline against the edge of the bank, promised to be the means of their salvation.

Blade estimated the bush to be five feet overhead. He girded his muscles, hunched his shoulders, and surged upward, his right arm fully extended. His fingers hooked onto a branch at the base and held firm. "I'm going to put you down," Blade advised his son, and pulled himself to within a foot of the top. His left arm uncurled and he placed Gabe on the rim. "Don't slip," he said.

"Don't worry. I won't," Gabe replied.

"And now it's your turn," Blade informed Jenny. He locked his right hand on the bush.

"What do you want me to do? I can't reach the top from here," Jenny said, doing the dog paddle.

"Climb up over me," Blade instructed her.

"That bush will never hold my weight."

"We won't know until you try, and we can't stay like this all night," Blade prompted her. "Give it a try."

Jenny snatched at the back of his belt and began to climb, shimmying up him as if he was a sapling.

Blade grunted and clenched his hands tightly. Her knees gouged into his back, then his shoulders, and with a little push of her arms she succeeded in grabbing the edge of the bank. She pulled herself up and rolled onto the grass.

"Made it!"

The Warrior hoisted himself onto the bank and rested for several seconds flat on his stomach, listening to the battle royal transpiring to the north.

Gabe was staring at the cabin. "Golly! Those things are trying to get inside."

Blade rose to his knees, dripping wet and feeling the chills again, and gazed at the eerie scene. He distinguished many amphibian figures moving about the Founder's retreat, their distinctive shapes discernible in the dim light coming through the windows and the door. Now he knew why there hadn't been any in the lake. They were all at the cabin.

But why?

Who was inside?

"You two stay put. I've got to go see what's happening," Blade said.

"You're not leaving us here alone," Jenny responded.

"Yeah," Gabe added.

"I can't agrue. Someone needs my help."

"It could be scavengers," Jenny stated.

"It could be friends," Blade countered.

"Don't leave us, Dad," Gabe requested. "What if there are some of those things out here?"

The Warrior glanced at the cabin, then at the woods. "I have an idea," he said, and took them by the hand. "Come on." He led them to the trees, searching for the one he wanted.

"What are you doing?" Jenny inquired.

"You need to be somewhere safe while I'm gone," Blade responded, and halted at the base of a towering deciduous tree.

TERROR STRIKE

A thick limb hung within easy reach. "Here we go."

"Up a tree?" Jenny asked in disbelief.

"I doubt those things are arboreal. Their bodies are probably too slippery for them to be good climbers," Blade replied. He placed his hands under Gabe's arms and swung his son onto the limb. "Hold on tight."

Gabe wrapped his arms and legs around the branch. "I won't fall," he assured them.

"Your turn," Blade said, facing Jenny.

"Promise me you'll be careful."

"Aren't I always?" Blade quipped. He stepped behind her, took hold of her at the waist, and heaved.

She nearly overshot the limb, catching it at the last instant and clinging for dear life. "Were you trying to put me on the moon?"

"The moon isn't out tonight," Blade said, grinning. "Climb as high as you can and don't come down until I return. If a salamander tries to climb up after you, scream your lungs out and kick it in the head if it gets too close."

"Don't take too long," Jenny urged.

"Try not to fall asleep," Blade joked, and raced to the north before he could change his mind. He didn't want to leave them, but he had to see who was in the cabin. As he sprinted, he heard the sound of breaking glass.

The mutations must be knocking out the windows!

He grit his teeth and ran all out, hoping he wouldn't trip in the dark and injure himself. A dull ache throbbed in his abdomen and his forehead seemed to be on fire. Otherwise, he felt fine.

Gunshots thundered in the cabin.

Someone was putting up a hell of a fight. He hoped the mutations wouldn't slay them all before he got there. His trained ear realized the rifles had fallen silent. Only the automatic continued to fire, and moments later it too ceased.

A woman screamed.

Blade reached the field and stopped to get his bearings. Dozens of amphibians were milling about the cabin, and there were undoubtedly more within. He crouched and drew his Bowies, waiting to learn if there was anyone left alive to help.

There was.

The salamanders tramped out of the cabin in groups. The first group carried a struggling woman. The second had a man in their arms, holding him aloft as they rounded the front of the SEAL.

Blade heard a commotion, and then the third group appeared. But they weren't carrying a prisoner. They were swarming around a massive man, a veritable colossus, striving frantically to bring him down, striking and biting in a frenzy. But they might as well have been striking a rock. The man barreled out the door with salamanders hanging from his neck, salamanders hanging from his shoulders, and salamanders clutching at his waist. His malletlike fists pounded right and left, always in motion, knocking the mutations aside as targets presented themselves. The thud-thud-thud of his stony knuckles making contact with amphibian heads resembled the beating of a drum. For every three creatures the man struck, one never rose again. The awesome power in those brawny arms was keeping the salamanders at bay.

Blade's eyes narrowed as the swirling melee came through the door and the man's features were profiled by the light. Astonishment rippled through him on the heels of recognition, and he straightened, gripping the Bowies. The man battling so valiantly was Samson! Blade sprinted toward the cabin. He didn't know how Samson had gotten there, or why, but all such considerations were irrelevant. All that mattered was that a brother Warrior needed his aid. One of *his* Warriors was in trouble, and no force on earth would prevent him from going to Samson's aid.

The first and second groups of amphibians had halted, bearing their prisoners in their arms, and were gazing back at the clash between Samson and their fellows.

Blade realized that Samson was trying to reach the man and woman. He saw Samson and the horde of amphibians come around the front of the SEAL, and affection and pride welled

TERROR STRIKE

within him. No Warrior had ever acquitted himself more honorably than Samson was doing at that very moment, and Blade intended to ensure that his friend's herculean efforts weren't in vain. He raced past the first two groups, who were so engrossed in the fight that they hadn't seen him coming, and waded into the thick of the conflict.

"Samson!" Blade shouted, and swung the Bowies right and left, slicing into the mutations with a fierce passion, relishing the combat. At last he was able to vent his wrath, and vent it he did, cutting and slashing and stabbing, slitting throats and splitting skulls and severing limbs in a savage exhibition of primal ferocity. The mutants attempting to overwhelm Samson were taken unaware by Blade's onslaught, and over a dozen were dead before the rest awakened to his presence. Some turned on him while the others focused on Samson, and both Warriors were nearly buried under a living wall of amphibian flesh.

Still Blade and Samson fought on, Blade ripping the creatures open with his flashing knives, Samson delivering punch after punch. Convulsing bodies littered the ground.

The group holding Tammy abruptly released her, letting her fall, and entered the fray.

Blade buried his right Bowie in an amphibian's eye, then planted his left in the neck of a creature trying to take a bite out of his leg. He shook a salamander off his shoulders and whirled, the Bowies arcing downward, cleaving the face of a foe to his rear. Always in motion, he pivoted and lanced a hissing monstrosity, then rotated and rent a leaping mutant from its throat to the middle of its chest. Moments later, while evading a lunging salamander, his back bumped into something. Expecting it to be a mutation, he started to turn, and instead found himself back-to-back with Samson, who glanced at him and grinned.

They renewed their struggle; only now they refused to be budged, standing firmly in position, each Warrior dealing with those amphibians that came within his line of vision.

Held in the grip of a dozen salamanders, Jared craned his

neck and gaped at the slaughter. He had never imagined two human beings could be capable of wreaking such carnage. Without warning, the mutations holding him simply let go. He toppled to the ground, landing hard on his right side, and pushed to his knees. The salamanders ignored him. They were piling into the fray.

Undaunted by the increase in the odds against them, Blade and Samson continued to flail away. The head Warrior gutted one of his bestial adversaries, while Samson caved in the skull of another with a blow from his left fist.

A hand touched Jared's right shoulder and he almost shrieked in terror.

"We've got to do something!" Tammy declared, crouching next to him.

"What?" Jared responded, relief flooding through him.

"Something! Anything!"

"All our guns are in the cabin," Jared stated. "Even if we get them, we can't shoot because we might hit the Warriors."

"Then what can we do?"

"Pray they win," Jared replied. And suddenly he thought of something he *could* do. It might not be much, but it was worth a try. "Stay here," he shouted, and ran to the west, bypassing the battle and the SEAL. Amphibian corpses dotted the space between the cabin and the van, and he had to step gingerly over them before reaching the doorway. Heaps of dead lay on the floor. He dodged around and over the mutations, hurrying to the counter. His right hand closed on the handle of the implement that might turn the tide: the lantern.

Jared hastened out, going to the front of the SEAL this time, raising the lantern to illuminate the spectacle.

Blade and Samson were still back-to-back, two pillars of power surrounded by bloodthirsty genetic deviates, slashing and slugging with lethal precision. Dead or dying mutations were everywhere. Fifteen to 20 of the creatures were pressing their attack as vigorously as ever.

Fatigue was beginning to slow Blade's reflexes when the

TERROR STRIKE

bright lantern light lit up the immediate vicinity. Several of the amphibians automatically stepped back and covered their eyes, and Blade took advantage of their weakness to strike out with the Bowies and split them open. He saw the remaining creatures start to back away and risked a look at Samson.

Just then the Nazarite broke momentarily free from the encircling deviates and his hands dropped to his Bushmaster Auto Pistols. Denied the opportunity to employ them earlier because of the mutations swarming over him and the press of combat, he now swiveled both barrels and fired, mowing down the creatures in front of him. He spotted Jared near the SEAL and scrupulously avoided shooting in that direction.

The rest of the salamanders bolted.

Samson went after them, shooting on the run, slaying every amphibian he saw.

"Kill them! Kill them!" Tammy yelled.

Blade took a deep breath and observed Samson's pursuit of the creatures. He wanted to join his friend, but his forehead was scorching and his arms and legs felt leaden. A weary sigh issued from his lips and his arms dropped to his sides.

Jared walked up to the giant. "Are you okay?"

"I don't think I need to worry about exercising for a few days," Blade said softly.

"Where's your family?"

"They're safe," Blade said.

"Thank God."

"Yes," Blade said, and glanced at the man. "Thanks for bringing the lantern."

"It was the least I could do."

Blade stared at the lake. Samson had crossed the field, shooting salamander after salamander, and was visible at the edge of the water, firing into the lake. "I intend to come back here soon and make sure all of those things have been wiped out," he mentioned.

"Don't forget to bring Samson along."

"I won't," Blade said, and grinned. "And maybe a couple of the other Warriors. Yama—"

"Yama?" Jared repeated. "Is he as big as you are?"

Blade looked at him. "No."

"Really?" Jared said, sounding delighted at the news.

"Really," Blade confirmed. "Yama is a little smaller than me. He's about the size of Samson."

Jared made a snorting noise. "I knew it," he stated morosely.

"What's wrong?"

"Nothing."

"Are you still looking forward to living at the Home?"

"Yeah," Jared responded, and looked at the stacks of dead covering the ground, then at the Warrior near the lake, and finally at Blade. "But I'm going to feel like such a wimp."

EPILOGUE

"I hear the Healers have given you permission to be up and around."

En route to his cabin from the armory, Blade turned at the sound of his mentor's kindly voice and smiled. "Hello, Plato."

"I also hear you're leaving tomorrow with Samson, Yama, and Sundance to exterminate any remaining salamanders," Plato said as he came alongside the Warrior.

"Yeah. I'm going to let them do all the hard work."

"I'm truly sorry your vacation turned into a fiasco," Plato stated. "Had I been aware there were mutations inhabiting the lake, I wouldn't have suggested the idea of going there."

"Don't blame yourself. I should have known better. I've seen more of the world than most of the Family," Blade said. "I just wanted to get away from it all. I wanted to make Jenny happy."

"How is she, by the way?"

"Fine. She's decided we'll stay at the Home the next time we want to be alone," Blade replied. "She's learned a valuable lesson the hard way. There's no place like home."

Plato grinned at the bad pun. "And how is Gabe?"

"As rambunctious as ever. The experience has matured him, which is to be expected. I was worried, though, that he'd lose his childhood innocence, his wonder at the world, but he hasn't."

"Children are often more resilient than we give them credit for being," Plato remarked.

"He isn't very fond of salamanders anymore," Blade noted. They both laughed.

"I've been meaning to ask you a question," Plato mentioned.

"What about?"

"The new couple we admitted to the Family."

"Jared and Tammy? What about them? They're a loving, caring couple, ideal candidates for living here. Samson and I both felt that way or we wouldn't have recommended them," Blade said.

"They're assimilating into the Family quite nicely," Plato agreed.

"What's your question?"

"It concerns Jared. Do you remember the day you arrived back at the Home?"

Blade chuckled. "That was only ten days ago."

"Then you should readily recall Jared's reaction."

"How do you mean?"

"I was near the drawbridge when you returned. I saw all of you climb out of the SEAL while the Family gathered around, and I couldn't help but notice a most peculiar expression on Jared."

Blade placed his right hand over his mouth so Plato couldn't see his grin. He'd talked to Samson about Jared and knew what was coming. "So?"

"So why did he start hugging everyone in sight and keep yelling, 'Midgets! Midgets! Midgets!'?"